RISE OF
NIMROD
FLEET

PART THREE OF THE
CONTINGENCY WAR SERIES

G J OGDEN

ISBN-13: 978-1-9160426-5-0

Cover design by germancreative
Editing by S L Ogden

www.ogdenmedia.net

THE CONTINGENCY WAR SERIES

No-one comes in peace. Every being in the galaxy wants something, and is willing to take it by force...

READ THE OTHER BOOKS IN THE SERIES:

- The Contingency
- The Waystation Gambit
- Rise of Nimrod Fleet
- Earth's Last War

ACKNOWLEDGEMENTS

Thanks to Sarah for her work assessing and editing this novel, and to those who subscribed to my newsletters and provided such valuable feedback.

And thanks, as always, to anyone who is reading this. It means a lot. If you enjoyed it, please help by leaving a review on Amazon and Goodreads to let other potential readers know what you think!

If you'd like updates on future novels by G J Ogden, please consider subscribing to the mailing list. Your details will be used to notify subscribers about upcoming books from this author, in addition to a hand-selected mix of book offers and giveaways from similar SFF authors.

http://subscribe.ogdenmedia.net

ONE

Two heavily-armed Hedalt warships surged out from the asteroid field and powered towards the Contingency One. They had lain in wait like ambush predators, using the dense sea of rocks as camouflage. Alarms blared out on the bridge, alerting the crew to the danger, and each of them ran to their stations with only seconds to act before the warships were within weapons range.

"Casey, get us the hell out of here!" cried Commander Sarah Sonner, perched on the edge of her seat, but the gifted simulant pilot was already well ahead of her. Casey maneuvered the nimble Corvette away from the approaching ships and shunted all the power she could scrounge into the engines. But the larger vessels had a head-start and more powerful drive systems, and she quickly realized she couldn't outpace them.

"I turned tail and ran like a frightened rabbit the moment they appeared, Commander S," replied Casey, sounding singularly unconcerned, as if they were merely escaping from an angry farmer who'd seen them trample his crops. "But they'll still catch us, before we can jump."

Sonner pounded her fist on the arm of the chair and turned to Taylor Ray, who was at the mission ops console. "What *are* those things? Find me a weakness, anything we can use."

Taylor didn't look up from the console, but summarized what he knew in shotgun bursts, "They're reading as Corvus-class cruisers. Fifty per cent larger than us and heavily armed; forward plasma cannons, surface turrets, ablative armor... They're damn tanks!" Then he looked over at Sonner and his silver simulant eyes conveyed his feelings as keenly as any human eyes could, "With Casey at the helm, we could maybe disable one, but two..."

Taylor's voice tailed off, but Sonner didn't need him to finish; she knew how the sentence ended. She swung the command chair in the direction of the tactical console, where her younger brother, James Sonner, was stationed. James had assumed she'd turn to him next, and the wait had been agonizing, like staring up at the blade of a guillotine and wondering when it might fall.

"Lieutenant Sonner, I'm afraid this falls on you," Commander Sonner began, ensuring her tone was formal rather than familiar. She glanced down at the console in the arm of her chair and read the countdown timer on the jump computer. Even with the dirtiest set of jump calculations she'd ever seen, it would still be another two minutes before they could safely escape, and the Hedalt warships would be on them in seconds. "Casey can't fly circles around those things forever, so we're going to need you to inflict as much damage as you can."

"Aye, Commander," James replied, trying to sound confident, but he was painfully aware in that moment of how fragile his voice was.

"We don't need to vaporize them, but if you pop a bully hard enough on the nose it might stop a while to think. Understand?" Sonner continued, "Just buy us enough time to jump the hell out of here!"

"I'll do my best, Commander," said James meekly, before spinning his seat around to face the main viewport and accessing the forward cannons.

It wasn't a response that inspired a huge amount of confidence in his sister, and when she glanced across to Taylor, she imagined that his fretful expression probably mirrored her own.

Casey's cry of, "Hang on!" brought Sonner's attention back into sharp focus, as the Corvette suddenly lurched to port, smearing the star field on the viewport into a blur of glowing streaks of light. "They're right on top of us!" Casey added, hands and feet working frantically to keep the agile Corvette out of reach of the pursuer's weapons. Shards of plasma flashed past, lighting up the bridge. "You know, it might be helpful if we shot back!"

"Lieutenant..." said Sonner, staring at the back of her brother's head and urging him to act.

James was frantically trying to lock on to the lead ship with the turrets, but Casey's chaotically brilliant flying was making it nearly impossible. "Casey, can you stop wiggling for a second so I can get a shot off!"

"If I stop wiggling, they start destroying us," replied Casey, eyes firmly fixed inside her pilot's viewport, "but I'll do what I can."

Casey brought the ship around and swung behind the trailing ship, slowing just enough to give the rookie Junior Lieutenant an opportunity to lock on. The chainsaw buzz of the port-side turret rattled through the deck and explosive rounds sailed past the wing of the Hedalt cruiser.

"Damn it!" cried James, and then the ship was pounded twice, as if they had run into a couple of small asteroids. The bridge of the Contingency One was flooded with smoke as consoles exploded and circuits crackled and sparked. Sonner was hit by flying debris, which sliced a deep gash into her temple, and was then thrown to the deck, as a power conduit next to her chair overloaded. The blast split the deck in two like a fault line from a massive earthquake.

Taylor darted over to check on Sonner as Casey veered them away from the trailing Corvus-class cruiser, narrowly avoiding another volley from its plasma cannons. He felt for a pulse, found one, and then sank into the command chair. The seat was covered in fragments of debris and metal, but to Taylor's simulant skin, it was no less comfortable than a feather bed. He checked the console in the arm of the chair; the engines were undamaged, but the jump clock still had a minute to run before they could escape from the two stronger vessels.

"Casey, try to keep the lead ship between us and that trailing cruiser; we don't need two of those things firing at us," Taylor called out.

"Aye aye, Captain Taylor Ray," sang Casey, changing course again as another shard of plasma flashed past the ship's nose.

Taylor looked over at James, who appeared to be staring at his console screen, as if in some kind of hypnotic trance. "Lieutenant," Taylor called over, but there was no response. "James!" he tried again, raising his voice to a shout, and this time James did look round. "Casey is going to bring us underneath the belly of the lead cruiser," he continued, locking his silver orbs onto the young lieutenant's tremulous eyes. "When she does, I need you to hit its engines. Set the turrets to manual control and use your instincts. This is our last shot to slow that thing down, got it?" James nodded with staccato jerks of his head and then turned back to face the console, but Taylor called his name again and he glanced back anxiously. "Take a breath, Lieutenant, you can do this. You have to do this, or we're finished..."

James turned again and started working his console as another series of quakes and shimmies shook the ship. Taylor looked down at his console and saw they'd been raked across the back by the lead ship's more agile turrets; clearly they'd grown frustrated of Casey evading their big guns and had decided to inflict death by a thousand cuts instead. He glanced over to the genius pilot, whose silver simulant eyes were fixed on his own, waiting for Taylor to give the command. "Okay Casey, do your thing..."

Casey smiled back at him and responded with her customary acknowledgment, before peering back into the pilot's viewport and grasping the manual controls. Immediately, the Contingency One spun over and soared beneath the lead Hedalt cruiser, in a maneuver that should have ended with them colliding with the enemy ship head on, but as usual, Casey's skill defied logic.

"Any time now!" Taylor called out, as he

watched the inexperienced Lieutenant frantically try to target the enemy cruiser, before the pressure got to him and he panic fired. In his mind, Taylor held his breath, though in reality he had no lungs with which to hold air in, and watched as the rounds danced towards the engines of the Hedalt cruiser. A handful of the projectiles landed on target, but it was not enough to penetrate the tougher ship's thick ablative armor.

James bowed his head and looked back at Taylor. "I'm sorry, Captain," he said before they emerged from beneath the belly of the lead cruiser directly into the line of fire of its aft turrets. The Corvus cruiser opened fire and the bridge consoles exploded. Taylor and Casey were both flung to the deck, where they lay, motionless; silver eyes staring blankly upwards.

James slumped down over his station as more explosions rocked the bridge, and bowed his head. "I'm sorry, Captain," he repeated, softly so that only he could hear, despite being the only one left alive on the bridge.

A second later the computer began to calmly cycle on repeat the announcement, 'Warning, damage critical... Warning, damage critical...' until its synthetic voice tailed off, like an ancient tape cassette playing too slowly. The main lights switched on in the simulator room and the pumps kicked in, whirring tirelessly to empty the replica bridge of smoke and dust. Consoles stopped crackling and the fissure in the simulator's deck plating closed up, as if it had never been there.

Commander Sonner got up first and dusted herself off, shortly followed by Taylor, but Casey remained on the deck. She had placed her hands under her head and was smiling serenely, as if relaxing in a hammock on an exclusive Hawaii beach resort.

"Come on, Casey, you can sleep when you're dead," said Taylor.

"I've been dead for over three hundred years, Cap," said Casey, opening one eye at him, "and so have you, in case you've forgotten." Taylor continued to stare at her expectantly. "Okay, fine, have it your way!" she conceded, springing to her feet. "I thought my death performance was the most spectacular, though."

"It's not a competition, Casey," said Sonner, gruffly, as she wiped the fake blood off her head, but then smiled and added, "but if it was then my dying act was clearly the best. Did you see how I threw myself out of the chair?"

"I thought it was a bit overdone..." said Taylor, trying to play it with a straight face, but failing.

"Am I the only one who doesn't find this funny?" asked James, who had raised his chin off his chest to watch the others banter together. His comment seemed to flip a switch inside his older sister, like pressing a button that flash-froze her mood.

"No, you're the only one who *shouldn't* find this funny, Junior Lieutenant," she said, sharply. "The rest of us have run this sim a dozen times, and we've all seen real action too. If we'd messed up out there like you just did in here, then none of us would be talking to you now."

James was torn between straightening to attention, as would be expected when being given a dressing down by a commanding officer, and flipping the bird at his bossy older sister. He chose the former. "I'm sorry, Commander, I will do better next time."

Sonner sighed and retracted some of her spines, "No, there won't be a next time," she said levelly. "You'll take the mission ops station and Captain Ray will remain at tactical."

"Yes, Commander," said James, glumly.

"Believe me, I'd rather we had the Captain's expertise at mission ops," Sonner went on, "because he's a lousy shot too..."

"Hey, that hurts!" Taylor butted in.

"But, out there we don't get a second chance," Sonner continued, ignoring Taylor's protestations, "and we don't have any more time to train on it."

"I understand, Commander," James answered, trying to sound more upbeat, "I won't let you down."

Casey waltzed into the center of the bridge, winking kindly at James as she did so, and then rested an arm on Taylor's shoulder before meeting Sonner's curious eyes. "So, what are we up to next, Commander S?"

Sonner pressed her hands to her hips and considered her response. In many ways, spending more time training was the smart option, and it also gave the new engineering crew that they'd recovered from the asteroid base more time to get the Nimrod Fleet fully prepared. But between their less-than-subtle heist of Casey and the black market transceiver from the Way Station, and their short battle with a Hedalt War Frigate, she knew that the Empire's eyes would be turned on them. It was impossible to know how much they really knew – perhaps they suspected them to be nothing more than racketeers – but if there was any suggestion that Hedalt Warfare Command knew something of the Contingency then they had to act as quickly as possible to recover the flight crews, before the Hedalt found them first. She made her decision and announced it to the others, "We caused a real stink back at the Way Station, but there's no suggestion that Warfare Command is on to us," Sonner began, "So, for now, we use every second we have to prepare. That means we train for a few more days, while we have the chance. But we've done enough for today; you're all dismissed for the evening."

"Aye aye, Commander Sarah Sonner," sang Casey, practically skipping off the bridge of the combat simulator. Lieutenant James Sonner followed, and Taylor gave him a reassuring slap on the back as he passed, being careful to measure the strength of the blow so it didn't knock him flat or crush any vertebrae. But as Commander Sonner made to leave, Taylor hung back, causing her to pause and look at him quizzically.

"Thinking of some solo training?" quipped Sonner, but then she remembered her dig at him about being a lousy shot, "I didn't mean what I said, by the way, you're solid at tactical; just not as good as you are at mission ops, or command, that's all."

"It's not that," said Taylor, trying to pluck up the courage to tell Sonner about his encounter with Provost Adra during his last jaunt through the Fabric. He'd told himself there had never been an opportune moment, but if he was honest with himself, there had been; he just didn't want to have the awkward conversation. Now he could no longer put it off, because if Sonner was choosing to delay the mission to recover the reserve flight crews, under the false impression that Warfare Command was still in the dark about them, then she needed to know this was no longer the case.

He fixed his silver simulant eyes on hers and said, "There's something I need to tell you."

TWO

Provost Adra's War Frigate ploughed through the asteroid field, bouncing smaller rocks out of its path as if they were nothing more than balls of cotton candy. In the center of the command platform Adra stood with her eyes closed, listening to the percussive thuds of the plasma turrets mounted all around the hull of the hawk-like ship pummeling the more threatening asteroids into dust. Unlike the incessant drone of the ship's engines, she found this noise satisfying. It was the sound of power and dominance.

"We are approaching the target asteroid now, Provost," said Adjutant Lux from his station between the two pilot simulants at the front of the bridge. "I have displayed it on the viewport."

Adra opened her eyes and examined the

enormous rock for the first time; though given its size, it would have been more accurate to describe it as a planetoid rather than an asteroid.

"Our probes have emerged from the cave mouth and confirmed the presence of a concealed base," Lux continued, before turning from his console to face Adra and await further orders.

"Can we navigate inside?" asked Adra.

"No, the cave entrance is too small," replied Lux smartly. "I am readying your personal shuttle. It is compact enough to navigate through the connecting tunnel and reach the inner docking platform." Adra nodded and Lux turned back to his console, continuing the preparations to board the asteroid base.

It had been several days since they had tracked racketeer pirates to the star system, believing them to be pursuing the rogue Hunter Corvette that had swindled them out of valuable contraband back at the Way Station. Besides the giant asteroid field, there was nothing remarkable about the system, but Adra was convinced that the rogue simulant and his female human companion had been here, and so they had remained, scouring the asteroid field for any trace of them.

The search had been impeded by the damage sustained during the battle with the racketeer reinforcements, but it had also allowed time for the ship to be repaired, and for Adra's own wounds to heal. But now, they were finally closing in on what appeared to be a hidden human base.

During the time spent conducting the search, Warfare Command had ordered Adra's frigate elsewhere, but she had managed to convince her superiors to release them from regular escort duties. This had been on account of their success in dealing with the disturbance on Way Station G-7J00, and also due to Adra's insistence that other racketeers were still operating in the vicinity. This wasn't technically a lie, since there was that possibility, but in reality Adra was simply buying time. It was a lie that might one day catch up with her, but she was willing to take the risk.

Adra's report to Warfare Command had also deliberately omitted any information about her suspicions of a new human threat, and especially the rogue Hunter simulant. She had simply blamed the disturbance on the Way Station, along with the theft of the Casey Valera simulant, on racketeer criminals and the incompetence of the base's former constable, Dhar, whom Provost Adra had brutally eliminated.

This omission was a serious breach of protocol, but it had been necessary. Since Adra had created the high-functioning Hunter simulants, she knew that the Warfare Council would hold her accountable should one of them malfunction and threaten the CoreNet. And she would not be able to hunt down the humans and rogue simulants if she was stripped of her title and her command. She had worked too hard and for too long to lose her elite status now. With it would go any chance of being allowed to pursue her study of Hedalt history on their ancestral home world; the planet the humans called Earth. The threat of this was the only thing that ever caused Adra to feel fear.

Her idle thoughts of Earth began to cause anger to bubble up inside her; anger over how the Masters had taken her race from the planet and pressed them into servitude. It was not enough that the Masters had denied them their right to evolve naturally on Earth as its dominant species, but by stealing them from it, they had handed the planet by default to the lesser, weaker, homo sapiens instead.

To add further insult the Masters had made it impossible for the Hedalt to ever leave the many outposts, harsh moons and worlds on which they were forced to serve. The shackles that bound them were a genetically-engineered weakness to super-luminal space travel, which made Hedalt brainwaves incompatible with the sub-layer of space they called the Fabric. If any Hedalt attempted to commandeer a ship and jump away, their brains would instantly suffer fatal neural damage. Only a freak mutation present amongst a minuscule fraction of the population gifted some individuals a tolerance to super-luminal travel. But even for these few, Adra and Lux amongst them, too much exposure to the Fabric would still lead to catastrophic neurological damage and, ultimately, death.

The only beneficial side-effects of the Masters' genetic meddling were the Hedalt's exceptional strength and long-life. These attributes were granted only because the inconvenience of Hedalt mortality had become bothersome to the Masters. Growing and re-training replacement workers every forty to sixty years due to them dying of injury or age was simply inefficient, and so the Hedalt were built to endure, and made to last.

Adra tried to push her anger towards the Masters out of her mind and focus on the task at hand, but there was no escaping the fact that the two were inextricably linked. The Masters may have been long gone, but their technology lived on. And it had been Adra who had given it life by repurposing their synthetic bodies and cybernetic components to create human-simulant hybrids.

Careful to ensure that Lux could not see her, Adra massaged the back of her neck and flexed her aching muscles. She was still in some pain from the multiple knife injuries sustained while fighting the racketeers, and her frigate was similarly still battle-scarred, even accounting for the running repairs. Taking such a massive ship into a dense asteroid field was a risk, despite the mass of its hull and power of its weapons systems, but Adra had to know what secrets were contained inside the asteroid base. She knew now, without question, that an element of humanity had survived, despite the Hedalt Empire combing the galaxy for over three hundred years to ensure no trace remained. The Warfare Council's belief that the human race was extinct had prompted their decision to systematically dismantle the Hunter Corvette fleet over a period of decades, so that only a handful of these ships now remained. But Adra had always believed this action to have been premature. Humans had not been eradicated, and the human brain inside at least one high-functioning simulant had become aware of what it was and joined them.

It was the simulant that concerned Adra the most. Humans were weak; Warfare Command had defeated Earth Fleet at the peak of its strength, and whatever pitiful revenge armada the humans might assemble would be squashed just as easily. But a simulant, awake to what it was, and in full control of the Masters' former ability to travel through and manipulate the CoreNet was more of a threat than a thousand Nimrods. The CoreNet was the means through which the Hedalt Empire maintained control over the army of simulant slaves that served its will, including those that were fundamental to the operation of its vast

17

armada of warships. That this rogue simulant – this anomaly – was able to manipulate the CoreNet posed a grave threat to the empire's system of control. It had to be eliminated.

Adra pointed to one of the halo of screens above her command platform and drew her hand to her chest, causing the display to swoop down on a thin metal arm. She examined the images that the probes had taken whilst inside the cave and felt a grudging admiration for the ingenuity the humans had shown in building this base under the noses of the empire. She wondered how many others there were still out there among the stars. Her musings were interrupted by a shudder that was severe enough to throw her slightly off balance. An alarm sounded briefly before Lux silenced it and turned to face her.

"One of the larger asteroids made it through our firing perimeter, Provost," said Lux, calmly. "We have sustained only minor damage, but the longer we remain the greater the risk to the ship."

"I am aware of the risk, Adjutant Lux," Adra answered, sharply, slightly aggravated by how Lux had stated the obvious. But she was unconcerned for the welfare of her War Frigate; she knew its capabilities far better than Lux. "Is my shuttle ready?"

"Yes, Provost."

"Then we will board this base and together we

will learn the extent of the human resurgence," said Adra, stepping down from the command platform and walking along the central artery of the frigate, towards the shuttle bay. Adra had chosen her words deliberately. To begin with, Lux had irritated her with his constant questions and second-guessing, but in their recent encounters he had proved himself to be strong, capable and, most important of all, loyal. And though he still occasionally overstepped, as he had done moments earlier, she needed his support. The longer Adra continued to evade or disobey orders from Warfare Command, the more perilous her situation would become. And though it pained Adra to admit it, she needed Lux as an ally. She needed his trust, not just his blind obedience.

Lux dithered at his station, slightly stunned that Adra had referred to them as a team, rather than merely as commander and subordinate. It was a small detail, but significant too, at least to Lux. He composed himself, before sweeping off the bridge in pursuit of his Provost, filled with pride and a thirst to prove himself worthy of her faith in him.

THREE

Lux piloted the shuttle alongside the outer airlock door and set the small ship down on the deck next to the main docking umbilical. Their scans had shown no indication of external security systems or weapons systems, and they had detected only a low residual power signature. As far as they could discern, the base had been abandoned in a hurry.

Lux sealed off the rear compartment of the shuttle from the cockpit section, before latching their docking ring onto the airlock door. Powerful cutting lasers then began to slice through the metal as if it were nothing more than balsa wood.

Without a word to one another, Adra and Lux got out of their seats and conducted final checks on their suits; a survival variant of the black armor that was designed for harsh atmospheres and even vacuums for a limited amount of time. A heavy thud reverberated throughout the ship and Lux turned back to check his console.

"We have cut through and established a seal," Lux announced, "there is pressure inside the base and the air is at a breathable concentration." Then, encouraged by Adra's earlier comment about them working together, he chanced an opinion. "If I may, Provost, I would still advise wearing our helmets until we are sure there are no toxins present in the air."

Adra glanced across to Lux with her sharp green eyes, "You suspect that the humans would poison the air?"

Lux nodded, "I suggest we take no chances."

Adra stepped up to the partition door that separated the cockpit from the rear compartment. "You give them more credit than they deserve," she said flatly. "The humans are arrogant. They would not expect us to discover this base." Lux was silent and merely bowed his head a fraction to show he deferred to Adra's greater wisdom. But, as with most of her exchanges with Lux, her response had been a test to check whether the young Adjutant would accept Adra's judgment without question, and she was pleased to see that he had. In truth, Adra shared Lux's view that caution was necessary. "Nevertheless, we will proceed with helmets enabled."

Though Adra had not said, "I agree with you," in so many words, the fact she had gone with his suggestion meant more to Lux than the stern Provost could possibly know. It was more than an acknowledgment of his input; it was an acknowledgment of his value. Provosts seldom offered praise, and for a subordinate to seek recognition was seen as vanity, something that was beneath the station of the elite officers of Warfare Command. Yet, to receive recognition from Adra, even for something as seemingly insignificant as her agreeing with his assessment, made him feel triumphant.

"Yes, Provost," Lux answered, before quickly pressing a panel on his wrist, causing his helmet to swoop overhead from its stow inside the armored suit. The full, black facemask not only sealed him from the outside environment, but also ensured that Adra could not see his prideful reaction.

Adra also enabled her helmet and then released the partition door to the rear compartment. The pressure equalized and Adra stepped up to the hatch opening, before checking the environment readout in her visor display. It showed a temperature of twelve degrees Celsius and an oxygen concentration level of just under fifteen per cent. Without their helmets and breathing systems, the low oxygen would rapidly accelerate exhaustion and inhibit mental functions, which was reason enough to keep them attached, despite the suits' sensors detecting no signs of toxins. Adra drew her plasma pistol and stepped through the hatch opening and into the base.

"There is a junction ahead," said Lux, reading the information on the inside of his visor as they advanced along the corridor. "The main section of the base appears to be directly ahead. I am detecting no signs of life; no movement, no heat sources that would indicate human life."

"They have already run from this place," said Adra, with a mix of disdain and irritation, "but the base may yet reveal to us where they went. Locate a command center where we can interface with their computer systems."

Lux moved ahead of Adra to allow the short-range scanners in his suit to peer more deeply inside the structure. Together with the data from their earlier probes, this began to form a simple map of the base. He focused in on what looked to be a large space on the upper level, but as he approached the door separating the outer corridor from the main base, a ripple of electrical activity danced across his visor display and then vanished. He initially dismissed it as mere interference or static, but then realized he was detecting nothing that could account for the source.

"Is there a problem, Adjutant?" said Adra,

noticing that Lux appeared to have halted.

Lux waited, his eyes flicking around the inside of his visor, but the interference did not return. "No, Provost," he said after a slight delay, concerned that Adra would think him timid and nervous for mentioning such a trivial detail. "I believe I have located an area that may serve as a command center," he continued quickly, not allowing Adra to question him further. "Through these doors, there is a stairwell in the center of the main concourse, to the left. My estimation is that the command center is on the second level on the opposite side to the stairwell."

Had Adra been able to see Lux's hesitant eyes, she may have pressed him further, but she was eager to enter the base and discover its secrets. She grabbed the handle of the hefty safety door, pistol held at her side and pushed through onto the concourse. Lights flickered on as the door swung open, but only enough to bathe the base in a moonlight glow, and other than the thrum of the lighting circuits and the sharp clack of their boots on the stone floor, there was no sound. Adra marched briskly along the concourse towards the stairwell that Lux had indicated, while the adjutant followed more cautiously a few meters behind, with his weapon held ready.

As Lux moved deeper into the base he noticed a series of scratches and pock marks carved into the dull rock floor. As he stopped and crouched down to inspect them his visor automatically displayed its analysis, showing traces of lead and copper inside the grooves. *Residuals from primitive weapons fire?* wondered Lux. But w*hy would humans be firing weapons in their own base?* He stood with the intention of alerting Adra to his discovery, but the Provost was already on her way up the stairwell. He hurried after her, feeling a growing sense of unease about the safety of the base, but then the electrical interference dashed across his visor again and he stopped dead, watching it. This time it did not vanish. Suddenly, an object swept out of the shadows from behind one of the stone pillars at the far end of the concourse and darted upwards. Lux's visor flashed red, highlighting the object in a white chevron and identifying it as an Earth Fleet sentinel drone.

Lux opened his mouth to warn Provost Adra, but before he could draw breath, he was struck in the chest and knocked to his back. He groaned and looked down to see a metal shard about the same size as his thumb embedded into his chest plate. He reached for it, but was then paralyzed by a surge of electrical energy. The jolt only continued for a few seconds, but the pain was more intense than anything he'd ever experienced before, even during a jump. The overlay inside his visor went blank and his helmet retracted automatically as all power to his suit failed. The sentinel swooped lower and Lux rolled to the side, narrowly avoiding another projectile that dug into the floor where he had lain on his back moments earlier, before dumping its electrical charge harmlessly into the rock. Lux pulled himself up behind one of the pillars and looked for Adra, but then he heard a distant, shrill scream.

"Provost!" Lux called out at the top of his voice, but the effort hurt his chest, which still throbbed from the impact of the electroshock projectile. Lux was familiar with these weapons from studying the archives of the war. Sentinels were a late Earth Fleet development designed primarily to attack and disable the simulants that crewed Hedalt warships. They would be injected into the body of Hedalt ships inside the shafts of disarmed torpedoes, with nose sections designed to puncture the hull like spears. Once inside they would fire their electroshock projectiles at the simulant crew. If enough could be disabled, the ship would no longer be able to function. The tactic was effective for only a short time before Warfare Command adapted and was able to detect and shoot-down the torpedoes before they hit their targets.

"Provost Adra!" Lux called out again, ripping the projectile from his chest plate, but there was no answer, and the communication system inside his suit was also offline. He peered around the pillar, spotting the sentinel, which was making a slow arc around towards him. He reached for his plasma pistol, but then remembered he'd been holding it when he was hit. Scanning the area around where he had fallen, he saw it in the center of the rock floor, tantalizingly just out of reach.

Lux edged around the pillar, using it to shield himself from the sentinel, and then he heard two more percussive thuds from somewhere above him, followed by the piercing screech of the electroshock projectile releasing its violent charge. Had it not been for his armor absorbing the burst, he would certainly be dead, and if Provost Adra had also been hit, she could be dead or dying too. He cursed himself for not speaking out about the interference in his visor when he'd had the chance. He now realized that no detail was insignificant, no matter how small, and his mistake may have cost him his life, and the life of his commander. Even if they survived, it would mean dishonor, unless he could do something to redress the balance and fix his mistake.

He took a deep breath and pushed himself upright. The air was thin and without servo assistance from his heavy armored suit, the lack of oxygen combined with the additional mass would slow him down. But Lux knew he was strong and he was sure he could make it to the pistol before the sentinel had a chance to fire again. He had no choice; it was either that or die.

He rushed out from behind the pillar and swooped low, grabbing the pistol in his right hand as another electroshock projectile skipped off the rock surface and embedded into a pillar behind him, before sparking into life like a firework. Lux skidded to a halt — his armor screeching across the grey stone floor — took aim and fired. The sentinel exploded in midair and crashed to the ground in flames.

There was no time for celebration, or relief, as Lux was alerted to several more shots coming from somewhere above him. It was the same booming thuds that indicated at least one more sentinel was inside the base. But then he heard the rapid whine of a plasma pistol in reply. *She's still alive!* Lux realized, before pushing himself to his feet and charging towards the stairwell. He made it only a few paces before stumbling and falling to one knee; his head was pounding and he was breathing heavily, yet no amount of air entering his lungs seemed to counter the weakness he felt in his muscles. More shots rang out above and he gritted his teeth and pressed on, forcing his legs to climb the stairs, each step feeling heavier than the last. At the top of the stairwell he swung around and collapsed over the railings; the short climb had felt like a mountain ascent.

He spotted Adra pressed against a pillar with a sentinel bearing down on her. He tried to compose himself and then held out his pistol, struggling to hold his arm steady. His hand wavered as he fired, sending a thin shard of plasma racing past the sentinel, missing by meters. He took another gulp of the thin air and fired again, hitting the far side of the pillar behind which Adra was hidden, causing the sentinel to halt its advance on the Provost and spin around to face him. Lux's eyes widened as the dread realization that he had now become the target registered in his oxygen-starved brain, and he flung himself to the deck as an electroshock projectile smashed into the balustrade beside him. He felt the charge ripple through the metal decking and surge through his body, sapping him of any strength he had left. Then the sentinel swooped over the balustrade at the far side of the balcony and aimed down at him. Lux closed his eyes, but then heard an explosion and felt the reverberant clatter of something heavy slamming into the decking. He lifted his head and saw the sentinel's smoldering remains.

His sudden reprieve from death had given him a burst of energy. He wrestled himself to his feet, hauling himself upright and again rested over the balustrade. He heard a voice shouting, but the pounding of blood in his ears dulled the words. His vision was blurry, but he could make out Adra on the opposite side of the balcony, also slumped over the balustrade, plasma pistol in hand, looking almost as weak as he felt. But once Adra saw him, she immediately forced herself to stand tall, before using her pistol to wave him over.

"Lux!" Adra shouted, before taking several painful gulps of air and then pointing to the large room to her rear, "Inside!"

Lux nodded and began to work his way around the rectangular balcony overlooking the main concourse below, while Adra staggered out of sight, into what he presumed to be the base's command center. The short distance around the balcony should have taken him no more than a minute to traverse, even at a casual strolling pace, but each step felt like he was trudging through thick oil. Finally, he reached the other side of the balcony and lurched towards the door to the command center, when he heard the unmistakable thrum of another sentinel approaching. Raising his pistol, he tried to pinpoint the sound, but his eyes could no longer focus. He staggered backwards and pressed his back against a metal door; he didn't know where it led or even if the door would open, but it was his only hope of escape. He reached down and as his hand closed around the handle the sentinel rose over the balustrade and bore down on him, hovering barely a body's length from his face. A raw instinct for survival took hold and Lux threw himself towards the sentinel, hearing the thud of its projectile-thrower engage, but his swift and desperate action had caused the sentinel to miss. He dug his fingers into the gaps between its metal panels and pressed his entire weight down on it, overpowering its thrusters and forcing it to the deck, before pressing the barrel of his pistol flush to its spherical metal shell and firing. There was a flash and Lux was thrown back against the metal wall, electrical sparks biting into his face and neck.

He tried to stand, but this time his strength failed him completely and he collapsed, eyes growing darker and his body more tired. And then his breathing began to give out. *At least I saved my Provost,* he thought, *at least I won't die in disgrace...* This gave Lux comfort and in that moment he accepted his fate. To die in service of the Hedalt Empire was no dishonor.

He wavered in and out of consciousness and then he felt himself moving. His eyes focused for a split-second, long enough to see Provost Adra's hand clutched around his boot, dragging him across the metal deck and inside the command center, before his vision wavered once again and he drifted out of consciousness.

FOUR

Commander Sonner paced up and down the bridge of the combat simulator, trying to sort through the mess of thoughts and emotions that were fighting for prescience. She was furious at Taylor for not telling her about his encounter with Provost Adra sooner, anxious to get out into space as quickly as possible to find the reserve base and flight crews, and utterly terrified at the possibility that the Hedalt War Frigate would descend on them at any moment and obliterate them.

"You should have told me straight away!" Sonner yelled at Taylor, still pacing. This had been the fourth time she'd yelled that at him.

"Will you stop yo-yoing up and down the damn deck? You'll wear it out," Taylor replied. During the short period of time that Sonner had berated him, his mood had gone from sheepish to apologetic to utterly fed up at being scolded like a wayward teenager who had just been caught smoking. "I know I should have told you sooner, but I didn't. I've told you now, so can we move on from this part, please?"

Sonner stopped and glared at him, "Which part is that, Captain?" she asked, still in scolding mode. "The part where you possess a simulant like some sort of demon, or the part where you have a slanging match with a Hedalt Military Provost and basically put a target on our backs?"

"The part where you stop talking to me like damn child!" snapped Taylor.

There was silence for a moment, and they glowered at each other with matching intensity. It was Sonner that again finally broke the impasse; she took a deep breath and managed to speak the next sentence without it sounding like an assault, "So tell me again what this Provost Adra said."

Taylor also lowered his hackles; it was easier for him to tame his anger, since he didn't feel the physical side-effects, such as an accelerated heart-rate or the feeling that one's blood is boiling over. He thought about the encounter again and realized he'd only told Sonner about when he spoke with Provost Adra, and hadn't started right at the beginning, from the first moment he had appeared on the bridge. "She talked about a signal anomaly in the CoreNet," Taylor began. "They were going to run some sort of signal purge."

"Right, you've mentioned this purge before," said Sonner, "They believed your incursions into the CoreNet were just some unexplained signal anomaly that needed to be eradicated, right?"

"Yes, except this time she told her lieutenant, the one she called Adjutant Lux, to hold off," Taylor went on. "She said she believed something was there; that something being me."

"They specifically talked about the anomaly as being a Hunter simulant?" asked Sonner, and Taylor nodded. "But why? What reason had she to suspect that?"

"I don't know, but she was talking as if she was the one who created simulants. She mentioned me, Casey, Blake and Satomi specifically," replied Taylor, searching his memory to remember. His body may have been entirely synthetic, but his brain was human and as prone to forgetfulness as any other. "And she said that Earth had always belonged to the 'Hedaltus race' too."

"Always belonged to them?" Sonner repeated, her face scrunched into a frown. "Why the hell would she say that?"

Taylor shrugged, "I don't have any answers, I'm afraid." Then before Sonner could flick out her claws again, he added, "But, I got the distinct impression that she had already figured out I was the anomaly even before I spoke up. Either way, she definitely knows we're out here, and is looking for us."

"Damn it," said Sonner, rubbing the back of her neck, "If that's the case then she could have been following our trail for some time."

Taylor scrunched up his nose. There was more he hadn't told her yet.

"What now?" said Sonner, "Don't tell me... you gave them our address and asked them to pop over for coffee?"

"She riled me," said Taylor, turning slightly sheepish again, "said I was worthless and made in a laboratory..."

"And...?" said Sonner, eyebrows raised as high as they could go.

"And I may have mentioned something about how they should leave Earth while they still had the chance," Taylor said, rushing through the sentence in the hope Sonner wouldn't quite catch it all. She did.

Sonner threw up her arms, "Great, so you basically confirmed that more humans survived and that we're planning to fight back. Why don't you just shoot me here and get it over with!"

"I'm sorry, but that damn Provost really got my goat," Taylor exclaimed. "She said I was more the enemy of human beings than the Hedalt are, and..." he hesitated, realizing how dumb what he was about to say next sounded, "and she called me, or the original Taylor anyway, an... imbecile."

Sonner almost laughed out loud, "Hell's teeth, Taylor, did no-one ever tell you about sticks and stones?"

"I know, I know," said Taylor backing down, "Like I said, she riled me. If I could have moved, I would have shoved my simulant fist down her throat."

Sonner shook her head and then let out an exasperated sigh. There was no point staying mad, at Taylor or the situation. It was what is was, and they just had to deal with it and move forwards. "You know, maybe it's a good thing," said Sonner, trying to sound more upbeat.

"It is?" replied Taylor. He failed to see how any of what he'd told her was good.

"It means at least we know," Sonner went on, "It means we need..." she stopped and corrected herself, "It means *I* need to stop procrastinating and get us back out there. We need crews for our ships, and we need them fast."

At that moment Taylor understood something about Sonner that he'd overlooked. Her prickly demeanor was a defense mechanism, a way to shield her emotions from the sheer magnitude of the responsibility she had taken on. But there were times when she'd lift the visor on the helm of her suit of armor and let others see her more fragile human side, as she had done at that moment.

"Look, you're not procrastinating," said Taylor, speaking as softly as his simulant vocal processor would allow. "Before, we had nothing to lose and everything to gain; we had no choice but to just roll the dice and hope for the best. But now, it's different. Now we actually have a chance of pulling this off."

"And it scares the hell out of me," admitted Sonner. But then, out of the blue, she smiled at Taylor, "You know, for a robot, you can be quite empathic."

"I'm actually a cyborg," said Taylor, returning the smile, "at least, I think that's what I am. And, you're welcome."

"I wish we knew why they hated us so damn much," said Sonner.

Taylor thought back to what Provost Adra had said about Earth always having belonged to the 'Hedaltus race' and that it was theirs by right.

"You told me once that there was a suggestion the Hedalt had been to Earth, a long time ago," said Taylor, recalling the conversation he'd had with Sonner not long after his initial awakening on the Contingency base. "Maybe they think they planted a stake in the ground back then?"

"Well, their claim is void," said Sonner, and Taylor could see that her armor was returning, piece by piece. "And it's about time we made them understand that."

Taylor nodded. It was time for them to roll the dice again. "I'll assemble the others in the briefing room. Let's go and find the crews for those shiny new Nimrods out there, and then kick those steel-skinned claim-jumpers off our land."

FIVE

The hangar was a throng of activity, with cranes moving crates of supplies and ammunition, Nimrod engines being powered up and tested, and engineers bustling around, working on a dozen different jobs in preparation for getting the fleet space-worthy. Spread across the three functional hangars the engineers had gathered all ninety-nine of the Nimrod-class cruisers that comprised the Nimrod Fleet. The hundredth ship, Taylor and Sonner had already sacrificed on the surface of the planet around which the moon containing the Contingency base orbited. It was a red herring intended to throw the Hedalt off their scent, should they ever stumble upon the system, as Taylor had before he was awakened. At that time, they had no reason to suspect the Hedalt were searching for the Contingency base, or even suspected its existence, but Taylor's experiences had changed everything. They now knew for sure that at least one high-ranking Hedalt officer was actively looking for them.

He stepped further into the hangar, away from the double doors that opened into the pilot's ready room and briefing area, where he and the others would soon discuss the next stages of their plan to get the fleet operational, and observed with deep admiration the indomitable spirit of the engineers. Despite losing Earth and their homes and families, and despite waking up three hundred years later to learn that the Contingency had never even begun, they were undeterred. It was nothing short of awe-inspiring and Taylor was frankly astonished at the radical change the base had undergone since the first time he had entered it. Back then it was a ghost town, dead for centuries, with all but one of its hibernating crew still alive – the equally indomitable Sarah Sonner. But the Contingency base wasn't the only thing that had undergone a radical shift since he had first entered the lava tube, then still under the control of the Hedalt programming, and still believing himself to be human. Since his awakening Taylor had grown comfortable in his new synthetic skin, and the more he accepted who and what he was, the more distant Earth seemed to feel. One day, he'd need to figure out where he belonged, but today was not that day.

He turned to go back inside the ready room, but then something caught Taylor's keen simulant eyes. There were groove marks in the deck plating about ten meters from where he stood. He wandered over to investigate, crouching to run his hand along the damaged area, which was also slightly melted, before he suddenly realized what the marks were. *This is where Sonner shot at me*, he thought to himself. *This is where I fell from the stack of containers and hit my head. This was where I became awake!* It was strange to think back on it. At the time, he'd seen Sarah Sonner as a kind of monster, a beast that the Hedalt had invented and tricked his simulant mind into seeing instead of a woman, as a way to make it easier for his mind to hunt and kill humans. No-one would think twice about killing a monster; children had been brought up on stories about slaying demons and ghouls for thousands of years. But the reality was quite different to these fairy tales. The truth was that he had been the real monster – a synthetic predator with a laboratory-grown, cybernetically-enhanced human brain, which had been programmed to kill.

He searched his memory, trying to remember those events again, but it was surprisingly difficult to recall them clearly, despite how recently they had all occurred. In his memory, the monster had been firing beams of purple energy at him from a plasma rifle, but the damage to the deck was consistent with standard Earth Fleet explosive-tipped rounds, not the Hedalt's more sophisticated energy weapons. He remembered back to when Sonner had first confronted him about what he was, in a room not far from where he stood now, and explained as best she could about all of the lies he'd have to face up to. It seem like a century ago; distant memories that didn't even seem like his own. He could remember what that earlier version of himself had seen and done, as if he'd seen it in a mission report, but he couldn't remember being him. He couldn't remember being anything other than what he was now.

"Whatcha lookin' at, Cap?" came the cheery voice of Casey Valera.

Taylor drew his fingers across the marks one last time and then stood up. "This is where I fell. This is the place where I first became me."

Casey looked at the marks on the deck and then into Taylor's silver eyes, which were somehow still able to convey the sadness that had been expressed through the words he'd spoken. At moments like these, Casey thought that 'simulant' seemed like such an unkind and inaccurate description. There was nothing simulated about their feelings.

"This is where you lost your crew, isn't it?"

asked Casey, and the question seemed to take Taylor by surprise. "You don't have to talk about it, if you don't want to."

"No, it's okay," said Taylor, "it's just that I hadn't really thought about it lately, what with everything else that's happened, including finding you."

"It's okay to feel sad about it, Captain," Casey went on, her voice sympathetic yet still somehow cheerful. "Finding me doesn't mean you have to forget about her. The other Casey, I mean."

Taylor smiled and looked at his pilot. She'd changed her hair slightly, pinning it away from her face, and she now wore a bright purple top underneath her Earth Fleet-issue shirt, which had three buttons undone, rather than the two that his other Casey would leave. On her feet she'd managed to find a matching pair of purple canvas shoes with thick white soles, though where she had got them from Taylor had no idea, and thought it better not to ask. But the most striking addition to her outfit was a necklace, made from what looked like a simple bootlace. Delicately attached to the center, tied in place at either end of the bow-like wrapper, was the mint that Taylor had found down the back of the pilot's chair and placed in Casey's jacket pocket, before she was awakened for the first time. He shook his head gently and smiled. He didn't know why, but this Casey felt more real to him than the memory of the one he'd lost. But then his smiled faded; he worried that the more time that passed, the less he would remember of any of them. He needed to find Blake and Satomi soon, before their memories became so distant that it would be like meeting strangers.

"You okay, Cap?" asked Casey, wondering where Taylor's thoughts had wandered to.

"I'm fine, Casey," Taylor answered, managing to resume a weak smile, "I was just thinking how glad I am that I found you." Then he understood something that had not occurred to him before, but that was obvious now that he was talking with Casey — the real, living Casey Valera. "You know, in a way, the other Casey — all the others, in fact — they were never really *my* crew. I stopped being that Taylor Ray right here," he pointed to the scorched deck plating that separated them. "You're my crew, Casey. And when we find and wake up Blake and Satomi, they'll be our crew too."

"Aww, stop it Cap, you'll make me cry!" said Casey, cocking her head a little to the side. Then she frowned, clearly a put-on gesture, and added, "wait a second, are we even able to cry?"

"With everything I've been through, I think I'd know by now!" laughed Taylor, and Casey joined in.

Casey then caught sight of Commander Sonner coming towards them from the hangar deck, her progress slowed by a need to return the salutes of the dozen engineers she passed en-route. Her brother, James, was at her side. "Here comes the dynamic Sonner duo," Casey nodded in their direction. "About time too, I've had enough of being cooped up inside this old cave."

Taylor turned to face them, but they were still some distance away, and Casey noticed that Taylor seemed to drift off with his own thoughts again.

"It must have been difficult for you to trust her," said Casey after a few silent seconds, "after what happened here."

Taylor thought about this for a moment and then shook his head gently, "It would be easy to be angry with her and to blame her, but the truth is there was no way she could have known," he said. "She was the last human being in the galaxy, confronted with four Hunter simulants who had been programmed to kill her. She could have killed me too, but she didn't."

"She can be real cranky, though," quipped Casey, "and more than a little uptight." Then she gave Taylor a gentle nudge with her shoulder, "A bit like another commanding officer I seem to remember..."

"Please, I'm a pussy cat compared to her!" protested Taylor.

"But she's got a good heart, and she's honorable," Casey went on, more solemnly, "also like another commander I know."

"Thanks, Casey," said Taylor. If simulants had been able to cry, he could have shed a tear right there.

"You two look like you're plotting a mutiny," said Commander Sonner as she arrived with her brother a few paces behind.

"Oh no, she's on to us, Cap," said Casey, ladling on a large helping of amateur dramatics. "Shall we take them down right here, or wait until we're inside the briefing room to assassinate them, as planned?"

"You know, I'm not even sure if you're joking," replied Sonner as Taylor smirked and James stifled a snicker. Then she spotted the damaged deck plating. "Are you wrecking my base already?"

"Actually, you did that, if you remember," said Taylor. "We've both been here before."

It took Sonner a few moments to understand Taylor's cryptic statement, but she eventually caught on. "Oh, right, yes," she said, clearly finding the situation a little awkward. Then she looked at the others and said, "You all go ahead into the briefing room. The Captain and I will join you shortly."

"Aye aye, Commander Sarah Sonner," said Casey, throwing up a lazy salute, and then she hooked her arm around James's and led him away. Taylor was sure he heard the younger Sonner say, 'nice shoes' before they passed out of earshot.

Sonner waited until the double doors leading into the pilot's ready room had swung shut behind them and then peered up at Taylor, hands on hips. Had she not been slouching, she would have actually stood a little taller than him.

"We never talked about it, not really," said Sonner, struggling to force the words out, but she wanted to give Taylor the opportunity to speak his mind. "I realize now, looking back, that the way I treated you, in those first moments after you recovered from the fall, was..." she hesitated, fishing for the right word.

"Cruel?" said Taylor, remembering how Sonner had propped up the dead simulant frames of Casey and Satomi against the wall in the room where she'd made him face the reality of what he was.

Sonner looked away, "I didn't know you then, Taylor." The use of his first name, rather than merely his rank, took Taylor a little by surprise, and his simulant eyes widened. "I didn't even know if there was a real you inside that synthetic head. If I had known, I would have done things differently." Then she forced herself to look at him and added, "I guess what I'm saying is, I'm sorry."

Unlike the memories of his life prior to the awakening, Taylor could recall their confrontation in the room where Sonner had bound him to a chair and interrogated him like it was yesterday.

The pain of it was still raw in his mind, if not his body, but as he'd told Casey, he felt no anger towards Sonner. In fact, in many ways he owed her his life.

"You have nothing to apologize for," he said, "you took an enormous risk in trusting me; a simulant designed to kill you. And you've taken similar and even bigger risks since to help me find my crew; risks you didn't need to shoulder. It's something I'll not forget, Sarah."

Sonner straightened a little, bringing their eyes level, and for a moment Taylor thought she was going to hug him. He panicked, wondering if he should hug her back, and for a moment his hands reached out towards her, but to his relief Sonner caught herself just in time.

"Good, well, we should get inside and start the briefing," said Sonner after clearing her throat with a little cough and taking a pace back. Taylor swung his arms up and folded them across his chest in a move that was intended to mask his half-attempted hug, but in reality just made his initial intentions even more obvious. Sonner mirrored his gesture, also folding her arms, and for a moment they both just stood there, mirror images of one another, nodding in agreement.

"Good, well, after you, Commander," said Taylor, in his best captain's voice.

Sonner returned his nod and then wasted no

time in heading for the door, "Good, yes. Well, the briefing shouldn't take long, and then we can get back out there, Captain." she said, before half-jogging away.

Taylor could see that her defensive visor had been lowered once again, but he didn't mind. The tension and awkwardness of that moment had been as unbearable for Taylor as it had likely also been for Sonner, and the return to normality was like someone opening a pressure release valve. He nodded again and, despite Sonner already being several meters away, threw up a casual salute, "Aye aye, Commander Sarah Sonner."

SIX

Lux felt himself being dragged backwards by strong hands that were hooked underneath his arms. His vision was foggy and his body still felt weak. Suddenly, the hold on him was released and his head came to rest on something hard and cool. It did not feel like rock, nor did it have the coarse texture of the metal balcony decking on which he'd blacked out. He took a gulp of air, but this time he could feel the oxygen beginning fuel his brain and energize his muscles. Whatever this place was, the air was richer than it had been in the concourse. Groggily, he tried to right himself, but it was like being forcibly awakened from a deep and dreamless sleep, and for several seconds his arms and legs just flailed around helplessly, until finally he managed to regain enough of his senses to sit upright.

He was on the floor in the corner of a room filled with rows of consoles and workbenches. It wasn't so much a command center as a workshop, Lux thought to himself. Provost Adra was a few meters away, leaning against one of the consoles and staring patiently at the screen. Lux fought himself back to his feet and slowly crossed over to Adra's side measuring each step carefully so that he did not fall. He would have preferred to have remained on the floor for some minutes longer, but he was worried that this would show weakness to his commander.

"I am ready to resume my duties, Provost Adra," said Lux, standing at Adra's side and straightening to attention, as best he could. The act of pulling his shoulders back stretched the burned flesh on his chest from where the electroshock projectile had impaled in his armor, and his body again flooded with pain.

A minute passed without a response from Adra. Instead, she just silently studied the constantly refreshing information on the console screen, and so Lux held his position and waited, despite the pain from his wounds growing with each passing second. It was then he noticed that Adra had projectiles lodged into her own armor; one to the right thigh and one in her abdomen, which was no doubt the reason why she was slumped forward.

His instinct was to check the severity of her injuries, to make sure that his Provost was not in danger of dying, but he understood Adra well enough now to know to keep silent instead.

Another minute dragged by with no words passing between them, and Lux's racing mind filled the void by fixating on his earlier mistake of not mentioning the interference he'd observed in his visor. Guilt began to overwhelm him and override his better judgement to remain silent and simply wait.

"I apologize, Provost, I should have detected the sentinels," Lux began, "It is my fault that we were taken by surprise."

"That may be so," said Adra in a cool, dispassionate tone that gave no hint as to whether she was angry with Lux. She then adjusted a setting on a device that was inserted into the console; it was something Lux hadn't spotted before, despite it clearly looking like Hedalt technology that was not an original part of the console's configuration. He leant in slightly to get a better look and then recognized it as a breaker; a device used to hack into secured computer systems and access the data stored within.

"I failed you, Provost," Lux went on, and though he tried to match Adra's cool delivery, his voice betrayed the emotions surging inside him. "You should have let me die."

Adra's eyes flicked across to Lux for a brief moment, before returning to the screen. "Yes, I should have," she answered with the same icy chill. Adra then rose to her full height, but continued to peer down at the screen. "You should have trusted your instincts, Adjutant Lux," she continued. "You saw something before we entered this base, but chose not to highlight it to me. Am I correct?"

"Yes, Provost Adra."

"That was a mistake."

"Yes, Provost Adra," repeated Lux. In a way, he was glad it was out in the open and he was willing to accept his punishment, even if that meant death. "I accept full responsibility."

"You are responsible for your error of judgment," Adra continued, "and so am I." Had Adra been looking at Lux at that moment, she would have seen the shocked expression that he was unable to mask. "I was too eager to enter this place; too eager to learn its secrets." Then she turned to Lux, hands pressed behind her back, and fixed her penetrating green eyes onto his. "Our task is too important to risk because of second-guessing or rash decisions," said Adra, "I will not make the same mistake twice. And neither will you."

"Yes, Provost Adra," said Lux crisply, but then Adra turned back to the console and peered at the screen again. Lux was frozen to the spot, unsure of whether his commander was still thinking about a punishment, or whether there was not to be one.

"This asteroid base and its human occupants were in a state of hibernation stasis for more than three centuries," Adra continued, oblivious to Lux's muddled state. "For three hundred years it remained out here, undetected, only for us to arrive mere days after the humans here were revived and moved out."

Lux moved closer and looked down at the console. The information displayed on the screen was fractured, incomplete. "They wiped the computer systems before they left?" queried Lux.

"Yes, but they were clumsy, and their methods are out-of-date, just like their species."

"You have found a clue as to their whereabouts, Provost?" said Lux, feeling a swell of excitement that seemed to wash away his pain.

Adra removed the breaker and reattached it to her belt. "A fragment of a clue," she said, almost smiling, "but enough to know there is yet another hidden human base; another tomb, like this one."

"Do you have its location?"

"No," said Adra, though her eyes had lost none of their sharpness, "but if they attempt to reach this other base, and the Hunter simulant that is their pet enters the CoreNet again, this device will give us a location fix." She tapped the breaker on her belt as she said this.

Lux nodded, "Then we shall have them soon enough, Provost," he said, also now rising to his full height. The pain from the electroshock weapon had diminished; now the only burning sensation he felt was a fire for vengeance. "We will destroy what is left of the human virus and rid them from this galaxy, forever."

Adra turned away from the console, before reaching down and wrenching the electroshock projectiles out from her abdomen and thigh armor, discarding them onto the floor. Each clanked and scraped across the smooth metal surface, briefly disturbing the void of silence, and then came to rest. Blood oozed from the holes in Adra's armor, but like Lux she was too filled with purpose to feel any pain. "Come, Adjutant Lux, we have work to do."

SEVEN

The briefing room looked like a university lecture theater, with a central stage in front of a screen, and cascading rows of seats arcing around the outside. With only Taylor, the two Sonners and Casey inside, it seemed unnecessarily large for their needs, but Sonner had argued that if there was to be a mission briefing then they may as well use a briefing room. Taylor, James and Casey were sitting on the front row of seats as Sonner moved to the center of the platform, holding a data pad.

Sonner cleared her throat and began, "The flight and engineering crews in hibernation on this base were intended to form the primary crew for the Nimrod Fleet," she said, tapping the pad and bringing up a plan of the Contingency base on the screen. "But, as you all know, I was the only one to survive." She tapped the pad again and a readout of the current complement of the base appeared on the screen. "Thanks to our successful rescue of the personnel from the asteroid base, we have enough engineers to get the entire fleet of ninety-nine Nimrods combat ready, but as you also all know, we don't have any flight personnel to crew them."

"I take it this is the part where you tell us about another hidden base?" said Taylor, who was eager for her to get to the point. He knew from his memories that the original Taylor hated mission briefings and the general formality of day-to-day operations, and this was something he shared in common with his long dead progenitor.

Sonner scowled at him and then tapped the pad again, "Yes, Captain, it is, and if you can avoid interrupting, I'll tell you all about it." Taylor held up his hands, palms facing outwards, and Sonner continued. "In order to provide backup forces should we take heavy losses in the field, or should this base become compromised, Earth Fleet Command placed reserve forces in stasis in two other locations." Sonner tapped the pad, bringing up an image of the asteroid base. "We're already familiar with the engineering base, which was to serve as a repair and refueling station for the fleet," she tapped the pad again. "The third base is different; it contains a reserve fighting force. Importantly, unlike the crew that were placed here, the stasis chambers on the reserve base were designed for a much longer period of hibernation, so that Earth Fleet Command would only wake them if necessary."

Casey stuck up her hand, as if taking the lecture theater setting a little too literally; Sonner rolled her eyes, before reluctantly giving way to her. "So what you're saying is that this third base is like a contingency of the contingency?" she asked, smiling. "A spare contingency?"

"A double contingency!" Taylor added, loving the fact that Casey's interruption had broken the monotony of the briefing. And, after Sonner's condescending put-down of him earlier, he was also enjoying the fact it had clearly irritated the Commander, who was massaging her eyes and the bridge of her nose with thumb and forefinger.

"A contingency so good, they named it twice!" Casey chimed in, and despite desperately trying to keep a straight face, James blurted out a laugh, which drew dagger-like stares from his sister.

"If there is a god or gods in this universe, I don't know why they saw fit to curse me with you two," said Sonner, who had now switched to rubbing her temples. "If we get through this war and you two are still in one piece, I'll melt you down for parts."

Casey scowled, but before she could say anything she would likely regret, Taylor stepped in, "Commander, I'm sorry, but the formality of the briefing just seems a little unnecessary. It's just us here and we know the drill. There's a third base. It has the crew we need. What do we need to know, before we go get them?"

Sonner looked down her nose at Taylor for a few seconds and then shook her head and sighed, "Fine..." she said, in the way that people say 'fine' when they in fact meant the opposite. "It's not like I worked for hours on these briefing slides or anything..." she said, haughtily, before peering down at the data pad and angrily swiping through the upcoming slides. Taylor, Casey and James all shot each other slightly guilty looks, but none of them felt bad enough to want to sit through another thirty minutes of Sonner's slideshow. The various slides continued to flash up momentarily on the screen behind Commander Sonner, until she stopped on an image of a dusty red planet with patches of azure around the equatorial regions. The image then rapidly zoomed in through the atmosphere to a rocky and mountainous section of the southern hemisphere. The image stopped at the mouth of a cave. Sonner tossed the data pad down on the table and turned to the screen, folding her arms in the process.

"The third base is located inside a lava tube, similar to this one, only much smaller," said Sonner, who now seemed as eager to get the briefing over with as everyone else. "It was never fully completed, but it should still contain what we need, which is around five hundred flight crew, in deep stasis."

"What about additional warships?" asked James, but his sister shook her head.

"There wasn't time. The plan was to construct more here at this base, but obviously that never happened."

"We need crews more than we need ships," said Taylor, steering the briefing back to the point. "The question is, how do we get them back here?"

Sonner reached over and tapped the data pad on the desk, advancing the briefing to the next slide, which showed two large, clunky-looking ships, both identical and roughly three times the size of their own Hedalt Corvette-class cruiser, the Contingency One. "The base should still contain the two large personnel transports that ferried the crews to the planet initially," Sonner said, pointing to the bulky vessels on the screen. "These will be sufficient to jump everyone on the base back here." Taylor opened his mouth to ask another question, but Sonner raised a finger to her lips to silence him, "And before you say it, Captain, yes I have considered the fact that these ships will not be able to jump along the threads undetected." She then nodded at James, who stood up and cleared his throat.

"The engineering teams have been working

hard to construct two new ship transceivers, based on the black market unit that is installed on the Contingency One," said James. "These are now completed and are being loaded into the cargo hold."

"So, the short-short version, which is seemingly the one you all want to hear," Sonner added, icily, while looking directly at Taylor, "is that we jump in, land and revive the flight crews, install the black market transceivers into the two transport ships, and then high-tail it back here."

"Damn, when you say it like that, it sounds easy," said Taylor. "What are we waiting for? Let's get to it!"

"I hope it will be that easy, Captain, I really do," said Sonner, more somberly, "but based on our record so far, I somehow don't think it will be..."

EIGHT

Casey initiated the countdown for the final blind jump that would take them to the system containing the third Contingency base. Thanks to the unregistered black market ship transceiver, they had successfully slipped through two Way Stations, without either of them contacting the ship to offer so much as a 'hello'. And, much to everyone's relief, it seemed that the racketeers were busy operating elsewhere in the galaxy, because at each of the remaining jump points they encountered nothing more hazardous than space dust. The final blind jump was another long one, taking them to the edge of the Cygnet Spur, where it was closest to the Norma Arm. Ordinarily, the task of computing each of these jumps would have taken several hours per jump, but Sonner's skilled and efficient engineering teams had helpfully upgraded some of the computer systems on the Hedalt Corvette, using spare parts from the Nimrod Fleet. This had helped to significantly speed up the process.

Casey spun around in her seat, purple canvas shoes pointed towards Sonner in the command chair, toes wiggling like flippers. "Jump ready, Commander S," she said, brightly. "Just say the word."

"The word is said, Casey" replied Sonner, a little wearily. "Though I'm glad this is the last time I'll be squashed out of existence, at least for a while."

Casey threw up a salute, swiveled back to her console to initiate the jump countdown, and then began spinning around in her chair again.

"Jumping in five...

...F o u r

...T h r e e

... T w o

. . . O n e

Taylor smiled as Casey's feet flashed past again and again, like a lighthouse beacon. It was a little ritual that was as much a part of the process of space travel as the computer calculations or the spooling up of the jump engines. And then she was frozen and the space around her and the ship collapsed to nothing as Casey, Taylor and the rest of the crew fell through a hole and into the Fabric, where they existed purely as energy, suspended in time like prehistoric creatures preserved in amber. But while Taylor would usually only experience the presence of the others in a disconnected sense, like feeling the warmth of someone's breath on your shoulder, this time he saw Satomi Rose. She was in a large room or chamber, surrounded by an array of alien-looking computer systems, consoles and what looked like stasis pods. And she was smiling as if she was expecting him, like a loved one would smile at a partner returning home after a long day at work. He tried to speak to her, but he was powerless to do anything other than observe. But then no sooner had she appeared, she vanished into darkness again, and Taylor's mind exploded back into real space, back into his chair at the tactical console.

For several seconds he was just in a state of shock, oblivious to Casey calling out that the jump was complete, or James giving an initial ship's status report. He wasn't even aware of the melody of bleeps and thrums and beats of the ship's many systems that constantly filled the bridge. All he could see was Satomi's face, smiling back at him. *Was that really her?* He wondered. *I was inside the Fabric, but not connected to it, like when I'm asleep. Or was I connected?* All he had were questions that lead to other questions, each as unanswerable as the last.

He considered mentioning it to Commander Sonner, but then realized that there was nothing really to tell her, other than 'I saw Satomi in my mind', which sounded a little corny and even embarrassing. But it was true that Satomi had been on his mind a lot recently, so perhaps it was normal that she'd occupy his thoughts, inside or outside the Fabric. He put the incident out of his mind for the time being and spun his chair around to catch up on what he'd missed, but the first thing he saw was Sonner bent over with her head in her hands, suffering from the super-luminal version of travel sickness.

"If we ever find an empty simulant body on one of these missions, make sure we take it with us," Sonner groaned, sitting back again, but holding her stomach, "I'd think I'd happily live inside one of those frames and sacrifice human sensations and physical emotions if it meant not feeling like this."

"Wait, you actually experience emotions?" said Taylor, grinning, "I thought you were more of a robot than I am."

Casey giggled, and James kept his eyes on his consoles so that his sister couldn't see he was also smirking, but Sonner just sighed heavily and looked at Taylor disapprovingly. "You know, when we recover the reserve crew from this base, I won't actually have need of you anymore," she said, deadpan and with a completely straight face.

"You'd miss me," Taylor laughed, "admit it!"

Sonner's acerbic response was interrupted by the shrill tone of the tactical alarm, which acted like an electric current delivering a sharp shock that brought everyone's attention into focus. Taylor swung back to face his console and saw that there was a large energy signature close by. In his daze over seeing Satomi and the subsequent banter with Sonner, he'd forgotten to check for threats after exiting the jump, and he cursed himself silently for being so careless.

"We're not alone, stand by..." he said as he hurried to assimilate the data. The energy signature was a scanning pulse that was probing the system, like submarine sonar mapping the darkness of the deep sea with sound. "Casey, power down the engines, now!" Taylor called out, "Run silent, quickly." Casey's hands moved faster than any human eyes could see and the background throb of the Contingency One's engine core diminished. He then turned to the mission ops console, "James, shut off the main reactor, and run on as little power as possible!" James had already anticipated the order and the light level on the bridge immediately dropped as the ship switched to its smaller backup generators to keep the fundamental life support systems online.

Sonner was already out of her chair and by

Taylor's side, "What is it? A ship?"

"No, not exactly," said Taylor as he worked his console and then brought up an image of the object on the main viewport. "It's some kind of space installation, and whatever it is, it's massive, and it's probing the surrounding space like a prison searchlight. We jumped in practically on top of it and were almost detected, but Casey killed the power just in time, so I think we're safe."

Sonner stepped back and examined the object on the viewport. Taylor hadn't been exaggerating when he'd said it was massive, but it wasn't a single mass like the city-sized Way Stations. Instead, the installation was built up of a sprawling collection of at least a dozen smaller structures, which were connected by an intricate framework of conduits, like a spider's web in space. But, unlike a spider's web where the strands become more densely packed towards the center, the middle of the installation was a giant void that appeared to be filled with hundreds of smaller objects. From the current magnification level, Sonner couldn't make out what they were.

"What the hell is this place?" wondered Sonner. "And what's in the center?"

Taylor zoomed in to get a clearer view of the installation's core. With the extra magnification, they could now see that in the very center of the void was an elevated, cube-shaped structure that was connected to the four quadrants of the facility via conduits. But more surprising was what the smaller objects that surrounded the cube on all sides actually were. "They're ships," said Taylor, zooming in even closer, "There must be hundreds of them."

"They're all in various stages of disassembly," said James from the mission ops console, "many of them have been sliced apart, like they've been dissected for parts. My guess is that this is some sort of reclamation and recycling facility."

"It's a ship's graveyard," said Casey, with a melancholy that was the opposite of her usual sunny demeanor. She looked at Taylor and it was as if she'd just seen a cat being run over in the street, "It's so sad, Captain. No ship should end its days like this, torn apart for scrap and left to rot."

Taylor nodded. To others, such sentimentality over what was just a bunch of panels, circuits and engines would have seemed ridiculous but, to Casey, space ships were like living, breathing animals. "Let's just call it a breaking yard for now," he said. "Graveyard sounds a bit macabre."

Sonner sighed and rubbed the back of her neck. "Well, whatever it is, it wasn't here three hundred years ago, and now the damn thing is orbiting directly over the part of the planet's surface we need to get to."

Taylor shook his head. Sonner had been right

when she'd said this mission wouldn't be as easy as it sounded. "Of all the planets in the galaxy, why'd they have to pick this one?" grumbled Taylor.

"I don't think it's just a graveyard," said James, but then he realized his slip, "sorry, Casey, breaking yard." Casey tipped her head back and smiled at him to acknowledge the apology. "I think this planet is perhaps a shipyard too. Or at least a manufacturing base of some kind."

Sonner folded her arms and turned to him, "Why do you say that?"

"There's evidence of heavy industrial activity and mining on the surface, and from the limited readings we managed to get before we powered down, I'd say the planet is an unusually rich source of rare metals and probably reactor ore too."

"Great, remind me to thank the genius at Fleet Command who chose probably the most valuable planet in the galaxy as a location for a hidden base," said Taylor.

Sonner dropped back into the command chair and stared at the installation on the viewport. It was a complication that they could not have foreseen, and one she had no idea how to overcome, "So how do we get past this thing? I'm open to suggestions."

"How about we slip around the far side of the planet and approach from inside the atmosphere?" Casey offered, "That way, whoever is on that installation is unlikely to spot us."

"It's a good idea, Casey," replied Taylor, "but if the planet is as heavily industrialized as James says it is, we'd have a tough time travelling across half the planet in atmosphere without someone seeing us, even with your piloting skills."

"Aw, thanks Cap," said Casey, picking up on the compliment, rather than his dismissal of her plan.

"The bigger problem is that if we power up, there's a good chance we'll be detected long before reaching the planet," said James, "and besides the scanning probe, there's also a perimeter sensor field enveloping the entire installation, sort of like a security fence, so a direct path is also out of the question."

"That's not surprising," said Taylor, "With all the tech and spare parts on those ships, it would make a really tempting target for racketeers and other pirates."

"We're still carrying a lot of momentum," said Casey, "We could just coast through the perimeter using the energy we already have, and correct our course with thrusters only. Even if the perimeter field detected us, we'd just look like an asteroid or floating debris."

Taylor looked at the data from his initial tactical scan, and shook his head again. "The perimeter is also protected by some pretty serious-looking turrets," he said, "again, likely put there to deter racketeers from trying to raid the place. We could try to slip through, but if they spot us then just one hit from those guns would end our day badly."

Undeterred by a second rebuttal from Taylor, Casey tapped a few controls and then pointed up at the viewport, "See, there's a ton of scrap and other junk already floating around out there. It looks like they just push their garbage out into space. I could navigate us through the denser patches, and maybe they won't see us."

Sonner had her hands clasped together and was resting her chin on them, listening to the various suggestions from the crew. Other than the alternative, which was to leave, she didn't have any better ideas. Returning to the Contingency base and using their new data to plan an alternative approach was perhaps the most sensible option, but Taylor's revelations about Provost Adra underlined the importance of moving swiftly. Plus, she was never one to take the sensible option. She glanced over at Taylor, who just returned a little shrug, indicating that he didn't have any better plans, and decided to give Casey's idea a chance.

"Okay, Casey, you're up," said Sonner, "but if we're discovered then we'll need to get out of here with considerable haste..."

"I'm plotting a reciprocal jump now," said Casey, cheerfully. "We'd need time to power up the engines, but unless they have ships hiding out there amongst the trash, I doubt they'd reach us in time."

"Damn it, Casey, I hadn't even considered that there might already be other ships scouting around out here!" complained Taylor.

Casey smiled and swung her seat back to face the front of the bridge, before enabling her pilot's viewport, "Don't worry, Cap, I'm sure there aren't any," she said, and then added with a wicked slant, "and there are probably no mines, either..."

Taylor shook his head at her and then concentrated on his panel, but all he could now think about was the possibility of them coasting directly into a minefield or being preyed upon by a hidden Hedalt warship, lying in wait, ready to spring an ambush.

NINE

Much to Taylor's relief, the junk field didn't contain any mines, nor were there Hedalt warships prowling the nearby space. And, just as importantly, Casey's plan also seemed to be working. Using the ship's momentum and the RCS thrusters to adjust their course, she had skillfully weaved the Contingency One through the mass of detritus so that they were now flying alongside the breaking yard and drawing ever closer to their goal of reaching the planet undetected.

They were more than half-way through the junk field when the collision alarm sounded, and a twisted hunk of some long-dead spaceship or space station spiraled towards them.

"Hold on to your pants, people…" said Casey as she pulsed the thruster controls, taking them directly through the center of the doughnut-like chunk of space debris, which was ten times the size of the Contingency One. The alarm grew more urgent as part of the debris passed by within meters of the ship's hull, and then tailed off and eventually fell silent.

"That was a little too close for comfort, Casey," said Sonner.

"I agree," Taylor added, gripping the arms of his chair and leaving little finger-shaped indentations in the metal. "Hell, I was pretty close to needing new pants, never mind holding on to them!"

"Thank you for that charming image, Captain," said Sonner, sarcastically, though in truth she agreed with him. She looked back out at the millions of tons of space debris still ahead of them and shook her head gently, "This is worse than navigating through that damn asteroid field. At least then we could shoot some of the obstacles in our path."

"It's going to get worse, before it gets better, Commander S," Casey called out, her eyes fully submerged inside the pilot's viewport. "There's a ton of junk ahead of us, and I'm not going to be able to avoid it all."

Taylor's tactical console bleeped an alert, indicating movement nearby, and he checked it, desperately hoping that their luck wasn't about to run out. He analyzed the data and saw that the movement wasn't a Hedalt ship coming for them, but something equally massive moving inside the breaking yard.

"Tell me it's not bad news..." said Sonner, who had also heard the alert.

"No, not for us, anyway," said Taylor. He punched a few controls and the image on the main viewport shifted to show an enormous crane moving along one of the inner conduits and repositioning itself over a ship that was dumped in the central void. On the end of the crane was an array of claws and arms and cutting tools, and Taylor, Sonner and James watched as it began to slice into the hull of the ship and pick it apart, like a vulture eating carrion. Taylor zoomed in further and then almost jumped out of his seat. The ship was a Hedalt Corvette-class cruiser, the same as the Contingency One. "It's a Corvette!" exclaimed Taylor, "Hey, maybe it's a Hunter ship?"

"Don't get any ideas, Captain," came Sonner's immediate reply. "Even if it is a Hunter, and there's nothing to say it is, it's unlikely there are any simulants still inside. Those would likely have already been..."

Taylor could tell she had talked herself into a corner. She was going to say 'scrapped' or 'reclaimed' or some other word that hinted at the recyclable nature of the simulant frames that Taylor and Casey inhabited.

"It's okay, Commander, I know what you mean," said Taylor, sparing her the awkwardness of having to stumble through the rest of her sentence, "and you're probably right, they wouldn't start slicing it up if there were simulants still on-board."

"Slicing what up?" said Casey. Her head was still pressed inside the viewport, hands and feet working furiously to navigate the Contingency One through the increasingly dense junk field. She hadn't see the grisly scene on the viewport.

"It's nothing, Casey, though it's probably best if you don't look," said Taylor, but merely saying those words made it impossible for Casey not to look. She peeked out around the edge of the pilot's viewport and saw the beast-like crane picking the helpless Corvette to pieces and her face fell.

Suddenly the collision alarm sounded and they heard the resonant thud of an object colliding with the hull, something large enough that the impact could even be felt through the deck plating. Casey darted her eyes back inside the pilot's viewport and frantically worked the controls, twisting and turning the ship away from the debris that now rattled off the hull like giant hailstones.

"Casey, talk to me!" shouted Sonner, but the pilot was too focused on steering the ship out of danger to answer.

"We ran into some debris," Taylor called out,

seeing that Casey was preoccupied, "but we're okay, just a bit dented, that's all."

"I'm afraid that's not all..." called out James, peering down at data streaming across his console, "whatever we hit bounced back into the debris field and is pin-balling off other debris out there." There was a pause, during which time Sonner and Taylor exchanged concerned glances, before James turned his chair around to face them. When he spoke, his voice was urgent and on the brink of losing control, "One of the larger ship fragments contained an unstable power core, and it's gone off like a flare. There's a ship heading this way from the breaking yard!"

"Taylor, can you confirm?" Sonner asked, but Taylor was ahead of her.

"Confirmed, one ship has departed the breaking yard. It's a small scout ship, twin occupancy at the most," he said, looking at the readout. "It's no threat on its own, but if that ship spots us then you can bet it will call in some friends."

"Either that or the breakers yard will just use its turrets to pulverize us," said James, and on reflection, Taylor realized that the younger Sonner's suggestion was more probable, and more deadly.

Commander Sonner glanced down at the console in the arm of her chair. The scout ship would be on them in less than ten minutes, and there was still a chance that it would intensively scan the debris field and detect them sooner than that. They had to prepare for the worst, but she wasn't willing to give up on the mission just yet.

"Casey, stand ready to run an emergency power restart," said Sonner, but Casey didn't answer. "Casey? Pilot are you listening?!"

Casey pulled her eyes out of the pilot's viewport and anxiously glanced back at Sonner, "I'm... sorry Commander, this is my fault,"

"Casey, get your head back in the game," said Sonner, firmly but without anger, "prepare for an emergency power restart, and make sure the reciprocal jump is loaded and ready. We may need to get out of here in a split second."

"Yes, Commander," replied Casey, though her synthetic voice betrayed the unmistakably human signatures of stress. "I'll make sure we're ready."

Sonner took a deep breath and let it out. Casey may not have been entirely human, but on an emotional level the simulant pilot felt as deeply as anyone she'd ever known. "For what it's worth, Casey, I'm not interested in blame, unless it relates to the damned Hedalt, anyway," Sonner went on with the same firmness, "You made a mistake. We all make them. I know you won't make another one like it again. As far as I'm concerned, that's all there is to it."

"Thanks, Commander S," said Casey, sounding

a little more like herself.

"Besides, if I what I have in mind works, it won't matter," Sonner continued, "Taylor, I need you to do your party trick."

Taylor spun his chair around and frowned. He'd been impressed with how Sonner had handled Casey's guilt over the accident, and how she'd shown an empathic understanding of her unique sensitivities. But, though Casey had blamed herself, Taylor actually felt responsible, because he'd inadvertently tempted Casey to take her eyes off the road, when he should have been firm and ordered her definitively not to. If Sonner had a plan to get them out of this mess, he was glad it would fall to him to carry it out, though what she meant by 'party trick' he could only imagine.

"Well, I do have a few tricks that I like to show off at parties, Commander," said Taylor, "but they're all terrible and usually fall flat. Which one did you have in mind?"

"I need you to enter the Fabric, disrupt the CoreNet and shut down that scout ship."

"What?!" Of all the tricks that Taylor had imagined Sonner might be referring to, that was not among them. "How am I supposed to do that?"

"You did it before, on the Way Station."

"Yes, but I was just making it up as I went along," complained Taylor, "I have no idea if I can do it again! And what if Provost Adra is still probing for 'signal anomalies' in the CoreNet? I don't fancy being 'purged', thanks very much!"

"You have no choice, Captain," said Sonner, with the same firmness she'd shown Casey, "It's either that or we jump back to the Contingency base. And if we leave now, and that scout figures out there was a ship hiding out here in the debris field, they'll likely plug this hole in their security and we'll have no chance of reaching the reserve base."

"Damn it Commander," said Taylor shaking his head. He'd wanted an opportunity to fix the mess, but Sonner had calmly shoved all of her chips into the center of the table without even looking at the cards she was holding in her hand. She was betting on blind faith that Taylor would deal her the card she needed to win. "How long do I have?"

Sonner glanced down at the console in her chair again, and then flicked her eyes back up to meet Taylor's shining silver orbs, "Five minutes... if we're lucky..."

TEN

Taylor raced back to his quarters so quickly that he had to grab hold of his door frame to stop himself hurtling past the entrance. Had he missed the catch, he might have burst out into space, leaving a perfect, simulant-shaped hole in the hull, like in an old Warner Bros cartoon. His grip on the door frame was so tight that it left finger-shaped crimp marks in the metal, but Taylor managed to swing inside and drop down on his combined bed and regeneration apparatus, as if diving for cover to avoid incoming fire.

Wasting no time, he enabled the regeneration systems and closed his eyes. Within moments he was inside the deep space corridor, staring at the starlight door. He ran through it, emerging into the CoreNet and its brighter and busier expanse of stars and glowing, wire-framed cubes that represented the countless thousands of super-luminal transceivers that made up the Fabric. Everything he'd done had been instinctive up until that point, but now he needed a plan to find the scout ship, and he needed one fast.

He didn't know how many of the five minutes that Sonner had given him had already elapsed. He wasn't even sure if time moved at the same rate inside the strange place he now inhabited. But his sense of urgency had also become heightened, because the CoreNet was uniquely the only place in the universe Taylor could still feel physical sensations of emotion. And chief amongst the physical emotions he was feeling at that moment were panic, anxiety and sheer, unbridled terror.

"Contingency One!" he yelled into the ether, and then he closed his eyes and thought of Sonner, Casey and James. "Take me to the Contingency One..." He felt the sensation of movement, similar to how the motion of the sea can still be felt even when indoors on a huge cruise ship, and he opened his eyes to see himself hurtling through space. It was still dizzying and disorientating, but he had become more used to it since his first terrifying experience, and he was able to remain calmer as the stars slipped by in silver streaks. He raced through super-luminal node after super-luminal node, until he re-emerged inside the deep space corridor, and the blur of motion resolved back into sharp focus. He was following behind the Contingency One as if locked onto its tail like a missile, watching it twist and jink and weave through the debris field. If Casey's piloting had been impressive witnessed from inside the bridge, watching the scorpion-like ship respond to her inputs from his new and unique vantage point only hammered home just how exceptional her abilities were.

Then he remembered about the scout ship that the breaking yard had launched, and he spun around looking for it, but it was like trying to spot a single speck of dust on a carpet. He closed his eyes again, trying to remember its shape and configuration from the tactical scans and urged himself to locate it. *Find the scout ship, find the scout ship and travel to it... Travel now!* But, when he opened his eyes again, he was still tethered to the tail of the Contingency One as it danced through the debris field.

"Damn it, Taylor, think!" he cried out, "How do I find that ship!?"

"It's called a Swordtail-class scout."

Taylor spun around and saw Satomi Rose standing in the deep space corridor a few meters behind him. Instinctively, he ran to her and tried to gather her in an embrace, but his body slipped straight through hers as if she were a ghost. For the brief moment that he had passed through her image, Taylor felt his skin prickle, as if he'd just been struck with an icy gust of wind, yet he felt suddenly hot rather than cold. The sensation faded in an instant, and he was left feeling foolish and embarrassed. It had been naïve to assume that Satomi was 'physically' there with him, because he only existed inside the Fabric as consciousness and energy, but he also regretted how clumsily he had given away his feelings for her. He wasn't used to feeling physical emotions anymore and seeing her had overwhelmed him. He turned to face Satomi again, standing tall and battling to hide his awkwardness.

"I'm sorry about that," Taylor began, "it was just a shock to actually see you in this place."

"It's okay, I know my appearance must have been unexpected," Satomi replied, looking down at her feet and brushing a loose strand of hair behind her ear. But when she looked up at him, Taylor noticed that she didn't look embarrassed; she looked worried. "I don't know how, but I knew you were in danger, and then I was here."

"Satomi, can you tell me where you are?" Taylor asked. Seeing her again had made him forget why he was inside the Fabric. "I mean, where your physical body is. Can you show me or give me co-ordinates?"

"Taylor, there's no time for that," said Satomi,

taking a step towards him. "The scout ship – the Swordtail – you must to act now to stop it!"

"But, how?" asked Taylor, "I don't even know how to find it." Then a more disturbing question presented itself, "Wait, how do you know about the scout ship?"

"I don't know... I just felt it," Satomi replied, throwing her arms out wide, "I think we're linked somehow. I sensed you when you jumped to this system, and just now, I felt your fear and your panic. I knew you were in trouble and it drew me here."

Taylor was about to ask how she had sensed him and how she'd travelled to the deep space corridor, but Satomi knew his curious nature and headed him off, "Look, none of that matters," she took another step towards him and reached out as if to hold his shoulders, and despite there being no physical sensation of touch, Taylor could feel a heat from the proximity of her hands. "You have to stop that scout!"

"Tell me how," said Taylor, "You said it was a Swordtail-class scout, but I've never seen one up close. I don't know how to visualize it."

"Focus on its energy, not what it looks like," said Satomi. "It's linked to the CoreNet, just like you, and everything that's linked to the CoreNet has a thread that can be followed. Feel for the thread, Taylor. It's close..."

Taylor closed his eyes. He could still feel the warmth from Satomi's proximity as he reached out with his hand, as if physically trying to catch this thread she spoke about. And then he felt a tingle in the tips of his fingers, similar to what he'd felt when he'd moved through Satomi, and similar to what he'd felt on the Way Station when he'd overloaded the power grid there. He could feel an energy, like a low electric current of only a few milliamperes, but it was enough for Taylor to focus on. Then like a fish being slowly drawn in on a line, Taylor pulled on the thread and suddenly he was moving through space once again.

He opened his eyes and Satomi was still with him inside the deep space corridor as the blur of stars resolved clearly again. The Contingency One had slipped into the distance, but he could still see the debris field, and just about make out the small shape of the ship as it continued along its chaotic path. But now, instead of being locked onto the tail of his own ship, he was fixed onto the nose of a small scout ship, close enough that he could see its two Hedalt operators inside, through the cockpit.

"They'll be directing scans at the debris field any time now, so you must hurry!" said Satomi, and for the first time there was a hint of her composure faltering. "You know what to do next, don't you?"

"I think so, but, I've only done it once before…"

"Then this will be the second." Satomi sounded considerably more confident in Taylor's abilities than he felt himself. "Do it, now!"

Damn it, here goes nothing! Taylor thought, and then he reached his hand out towards the small Swordtail-class scout, and was surprised to feel the energy of the ship start to flow through him. Then a jumble of white noise penetrated his mind, like a detuned radio with the volume cranked up, before slowly the sounds condensed and he heard voices; the voices of the two Hedalt crew inside the ship. He could hear them complaining about the pointlessness of being sent out to investigate junk, and what they would do once they got back, and he could see them adjusting the ship's controls and focusing scans on the area close to where the Contingency One lurked inside the debris field. They were close, but they had not yet detected the ship. He concentrated on the energy flowing through the sensor circuits and felt it flowing through him, and then he closed his eyes one last time and said, "Overload..."

A raw, visceral pain scorched through his temples and his eyes stung as if soap had been rubbed into them, but he managed to prize them open for long enough to see that the scout ship was now in serious trouble. Electricity crackled along its length, tearing open sections of the hull as the surge of power erupted through conduits that could no longer contain it. Its engines had failed and the lights inside the cabin had gone out, yet in the brief flashes of illumination from the internal sparks and flames, Taylor could see the two Hedalt inside panicking and reaching for fire suppression devices and emergency respirators. Then the gravity inside the little scout failed and the two crew began floating inside, as utterly helpless as the ship itself.

"I did it!" cried Taylor, turning back to Satomi, but she was no longer there. He ran along the corridor, away from the scout, calling her name, but she had gone, vanished back to wherever she had come from; a place that he still did not know. He should have felt dejected, but he didn't, and this wasn't because of his success in disabling the scout ship. This time Satomi had known him. She had remembered him, and what they had discussed during previous encounters. And she had come to him – she was linked to him. How, why, were questions that still burned in his mind as brightly as the fires that engulfed the ship floundering in space behind him. But one thing seemed clear; inside the Fabric, inside the deep space corridor, Satomi was already freed from the grip of the Hedalt Empire. He had to find her, not inside this place of thought and energy, but in the outside world, and he vowed in that instant that he would never give up the search.

ELEVEN

The simulant's eyes had been fixed on the console screen persistently for the last eight hours, and in that time it had remained so still that it could have been mistaken for a mannequin in a store window. Eight hours previously, it had taken over from another identical unit that had watched the same console with the same unwavering diligence until it had been required to regenerate. A third unit stood ready to take over, and so it would continue until Adra found what she was looking for. It was only a matter of time, she reasoned. Sooner or later the rogue Hunter simulant would enter the CoreNet again and lead her directly to the hidden human base. And then she would destroy it and all the remaining humans in the galaxy. This time, it would be for good. This time it would be their extinction.

Slotted into the main interface of the console in front of the simulant was Adra's spider-like breaker, the device which contained the fragments of data recovered from the asteroid base. Amongst this information were clues to the location of another hidden human refuge. The breaker's only purpose, along with the simulant that monitored it, was to detect and decipher the location of the unique signal anomaly that indicated an incursion into the CoreNet. If the rogue Hunter simulant entered the Fabric at any point inside the radius defined by the breaker, she would be able to locate the star system where the incursion took place with pinpoint precision.

The console flashed and the breaker sparked into life as new data was fed through it. Moments later the screen changed to a three dimensional map of the galaxy with a single white lane, tracing a path from one super-luminal node to another, until eventually the line branched away and stopped. The end of the line was a star system close to the intersection of a major spiral arm and a prominent minor structure. The simulant absorbed the information and sent a brief message to Adjutant Lux's console.

Lux was standing at his station at the front of the bridge, peering out into the emptiness of space with his hands clasped together at the small of his back. He glanced down as his console softly bleeped an alert and read the text twice to be certain, before hurriedly bringing up the new navigation data on the screen. He frowned at the information and then accessed the data himself, checking that the location was correct. Though Lux did not display the same scornful disregard for simulants as Provost Adra did, he still considered just as inferior and abhorrent as she did, and he did not trust the simulant's analysis. He glanced back at the automaton who had reported the data, looking at it with the sort of contempt a judge might show for a convicted murderer, before running the analysis again personally to confirm. *A simulant cannot be certain of anything, because they are nothing. Just as the humans will soon be.* Lux said to himself as the data continued to process.

The computations finished and Lux stared down at the result again, still struggling to believe what his eyes were showing him. *Surely, a mistake?* he told himself, but he had run the numbers himself and the result was identical. Lux believed in data. Unlike incompetent constables, racketeers and especially human beings, data did not lie. He trusted data implicitly, as he also implicitly trusted his commander and the purpose of their mission. Lux initiated the jump calculations to the new location provided by the breaker and then sent a message to Provost Adra, who had reluctantly retired to her personal quarters to convalesce.

Less than a minute later, the wide circular doors to the bridge swung open and Adra marched through, bustling with energy and purpose. Her personal suite was close to the bridge, yet Lux was still surprised at how quickly she had arrived.

"Report, Adjutant Lux," Adra commanded as she stepped onto her command platform with an urgency that matched her furious pace.

"The anomaly has been detected and its location has been pinpointed," said Lux as Adra quickly drew down one of the halo of screens above the command platform to inspect the information for herself.

"Is this data confirmed?" queried Adra, reacting in the same way Lux had done only moments earlier.

"It is confirmed, Provost," replied Lux, confidently, knowing that he had already checked the calculations and determined that there was no error. "The signal anomaly originated from a system containing a high-security reclamation facility, Cygnus G7-530. It is located nine point two five kiloparsecs from the humans' home star."

"From the *Hedaltus* home star," Adra corrected, but without malice.

"Apologies, Provost," replied Lux, but Adra did not respond, and was instead consumed with assimilating the data on the screen in front of her.

"But why this system?" commented Adra, more to herself than to Lux. "Cygnus G7-530 is heavily guarded. What do they want there?" Adra was struggling to comprehend why the anomaly indicated this one specific system out of the billions in the galaxy. She did not believe in coincidence – for her, there must be a cause for every effect – but it seemed highly improbable that the humans and Hedalt would construct facilities in the same star system purely by chance. There had to be another reason, but she could not see it, and it vexed her.

"Does the reclamation facility at Cygnus G7-530 process Hunter Corvettes?" asked Lux, not taking the chance that Adra's questions were not directed at him.

Adra peered around the side of her screen. "Yes. Of what importance is that?"

"The rogue simulant and the human woman have previously demonstrated a desire to capture other Hunter simulants. The Casey Valera unit from Way Station G-7J00, for example. Perhaps they are trying to rescue other units?"

This had not occurred to Adra, but the suggestion made sense, and aligned with the weak sentimentality that crippled all human minds, whether natural or grown in a lab. She brushed her screen off to one side and pressed her hands behind her back. Lux's explanation, though mere supposition, provided the logical answer she needed.

"Your analysis has merit." This was the closest to giving praise that Adra had ever come, and Lux very nearly smiled. "We must jump to the system immediately, before they have an opportunity to escape."

Lux nodded and then transferred his pre-calculated jump program to Adra's screen. "We can reach the reclamation facility in three jumps if we extend to maximum jump range," explained Lux, "I have plotted the first jump and the ship will be ready momentarily."

"No, that will take too long," said Adra, who had already reviewed Lux's proposed jump route. She pulled her screen back towards her and adjusted Lux's jump program, plotting a direct course from their current location to Cygnus G7-530, before processing the new set of jump calculations. She waited impatiently as the new jump program executed, aware that Lux was hovering in her peripheral vision, also eagerly awaiting her proposed solution. Finally, the calculations were complete and the corners of Adra's thin lips curled into the genesis of a smile, before her mouth straightened like an arrow once more. She sent the calculations to Lux's screen. "Plot this course, and initiate when ready."

Lux turned to review the new jump program,

which initially made no sense to him. He briefly considered questioning Adra's command, but then he finally understood what she was proposing and his heart began to race. He turned back to his commander to confirm her order, risking her wrath in order to be certain it was what she really wanted to do.

"If I may confirm, Provost... your course indicates a double jump?" Adra merely nodded. Blood was pounding in Lux's ears, but he controlled his response, "At once, Provost," he said, before turning back to face the front of the bridge and sucking in a sharp intake of breath. He knocked the primary pilot simulant on the shoulder, a little harder than he'd intended, due to the adrenaline surging in his body, and then tried to prepare himself, mentally and physically, for the ordeal that was to come.

A double jump was a highly dangerous and arguably reckless maneuver, made ten times more precarious for the Hedaltus race, due to its genetic frailty to super-luminal travel. A double jump involved travelling along a thread of the Fabric to a super-luminal node at the furthest extremes of the ship's jump range, pushing the jump engines to the limit of their capabilities. This alone was risky enough – if the jump engines failed mid-jump, the ship would implode and be consumed by the Fabric; converted to pure energy. But even if they survived the first jump, the next stage was just as harrowing. Rather than return fully to normal space, the jump computer would immediately initiate a second jump, carrying forward the energy of the primary jump, like skimming a flat stone across the surface of smooth lake water. The second jump was blind, but like landing on a trampoline from a great height, it had the effect of spring-boarding the ship a tremendous distance, far in excess of a regular jump, all in one seamless maneuver. However, the risk of serious damage was great, even for a ship as strong and powerful as Adra's War Frigate. But the risk to their own minds and bodies was even greater. Both Adra and Lux carried the genetic mutation that allowed them to endure super-luminal jumps, and both were mentally and physically amongst the elite of Warfare Command. But even for them the immense strain of a double jump risked more than mere injury – it risked death.

The pilot simulant indicated that the jump was ready and Lux anxiously reviewed the ship's status on his console. Warning chevrons flashed beside every primary system, along with a message that simply read, 'Discontinue jump. High Risk of Fatal Exposure.' Lux clenched his teeth and hesitantly cleared all of the warnings, before turning to face Provost Adra, "The jump is ready, Provost," he announced, somehow managing to sound calm and unconcerned, despite being wracked with fear and apprehension.

Adra waved her screen away, aware that Lux was still facing her. She knew what he would be thinking, and also knew he would not challenge her on it. But she realized what she was demanding of him. Previously, she would not have given a nanosecond of thought to his feelings or even his safety, but Lux had proven to be a surprisingly loyal and committed adjutant. This was in spite of Adra's flagrant and serious breaches of regulations, which would also potentially impact on his own future. He had earned her respect, something few others had ever come close to. Adra stepped down from the command platform and stood in front of Lux, and though she still towered over him, she met his eyes on a more equal footing than she had ever done before.

"I will not pretend that this action does not present great risk, to both of us," Adra began, "but we must ensure that we arrive before the humans and their rogue simulant pets flee once again."

"I understand, Provost Adra," said Lux. Adra's gesture of stepping down from the command platform had not been lost on him, and though it did nothing to assuage his fears, it gave him courage enough to face them. "We will catch them off guard, and force them to reveal everything. Victory will soon be yours. I am with you."

"Then jump when ready," said Adra, holding his eyes for a moment longer, before returning to the center of the command platform. She briefly considered moving to one of the side consoles, or to another location on the bridge where she would be able to steady herself against the torture that would soon grip her mind and body. But the reality was that there was nowhere on the ship where she could escape the consequences of what they were about to do. If she was to fall then she would do it where she belonged – on the command platform with nothing to support her but her strength and the power of her will.

Lux positioned himself at his station between the two pilot simulants and took several long breaths, drawing them in slowly and letting them out with the same measure of control. Then he dug in his heels and tapped the primary pilot simulant on the shoulder with the back of his hand, aware and ashamed that it was trembling slightly, despite all his attempts to steady his nerves. He then watched as the jump counter ran down, and with each changing second his heart-rate climbed higher and higher.

Five...

Four...

Three...

Two...

One...

TWELVE

The War Frigate dropped into the Fabric and Adjutant Lux collapsed into darkness, where he experienced only disembodied consciousness and an unbearable, unyielding sensation of pain. It was if his entire existence had been distilled down to millions of exposed nerves. The agony built and built and just when it seemed like it would never end the bridge finally began to materialize. He could feel his body again, if only through the pain that flooded into his bones and limbs and muscles like water gushing from a dam. But no sooner had reality begun to assert itself than he was squashed into oblivion again. Except this time the pain followed him and was multiplied ten-fold. There was no release mechanism; no way to scream or to bite down or even to pass out – it just existed and there was no option other than to endure it.

There was a bright flash and Lux felt his head land heavily on something solid, but there was no additional pain. It was simply not possible to be in any more agony than he already was. Slowly, sensations other than pain began to return to his extremities, and the shrill whistle that pierced his ears and mind began to give way to other sounds. His eyes pulsed in and out of focus, but he could see well enough to realize that his face was resting against a console. He pushed himself away, hands slipping on something wet and sticky. He held a hand up to his face and saw that it was covered in blood. He heard a voice, but could not make out the words. He turned, trying to place the sound but his legs gave way from under him and he slid down against the console, clawing desperately with his hands to find purchase on anything that would prevent a humiliating fall. Above him to either side were the anonymous faces of the two pilot simulants, oblivious to his suffering and injury, mindlessly staring out at the viewport ahead of them.

"Lux!"

He heard the shout clearly this time and felt hands clasped underneath his arms, hoisting him up. Other sounds registered in his ears and he rubbed them, trying to clear the ringing, but his fingers came away smeared with red once again.

He blinked blood from his eyes and looked into the face of Provost Adra, bleeding from her eyes, nose and ears. She looked half dead, but still had twice the strength that he did.

"Lux, can you hear me?" asked Adra, forcing her Adjutant to stand. Then she guided his blood-soaked hands to the metal frames of the two pilot's chairs. Lux grabbed them automatically, in the same way a baby might instinctively grip a rattle if it were placed in her hand. "We're here, Lux. We made it!" shouted Adra, her voice triumphant.

Lux coughed and then spat blood onto Adra's armored jacket, "Apologies Provost," he spluttered weakly, mortified and ashamed of himself for not being as strong as she was.

Adra released her hold on Lux and then dragged the secondary pilot simulant from its seat, an act that took a hundred times more effort than it would normally have required from her. Then she grabbed Lux by the waist and lowered him into the seat. An adjutant would never normally be permitted to sit in the presence of a provost, but Adra had demonstrated a disregard for protocol before, and this was no exception.

"I... am... ready... for duty... Provost," Lux protested, trying desperately to stand, but there was no strength in his muscles. Blood dripped from his eyes and nose and splashed across the armor plating on his thighs, as Adra pressed him back into the seat, where he finally gave up and let himself go limp.

Adra left Lux and staggered to a nearby console, barging the simulant stationed there out of her way, while other simulants ran around the bridge, working frantically to repair the damage, the extent of which Adra was not even aware. She input commands with blood-stained fingers and waited for the results to appear, but she was met only with error messages and warnings about critical systems. All she knew for sure was that they were in the correct system – the navigation computer had confirmed that much – but beyond this she was blind. If the rogue Hunter Corvette was in the system, she had no way of knowing.

Adra pounded the console with the bottom of her fists and staggered back in front of the viewport. Displayed on the giant screen, which flickered and crackled with interference, was a barren-looking planet, and in the foreground was the reclamation facility. *You are here somewhere, I know it!* thought Adra. *But you will not escape me again.* Then out of the corner of her eye, she saw Lux slide backwards and fall from the secondary pilot's chair, landing on the deck like a freshly slaughtered animal.

Adra watched Lux's quivering body for a second and then stepped back onto her command platform, each step feeling like a knife was being stabbed into her legs. "I want sensors online, now!" she roared, addressing the anonymous simulants as a collective. "And get me to that reclamation facility!" Blood splattered across the faces of passing simulants as she screamed words into the open air. "All simulants online, now! Repair this ship!" Suddenly the bridge door swung open and another ten simulants ran inside, rushing to various stations, or pulling open panels and disappearing into the guts of the enormous vessel. One ran towards Adra, heading for a damaged station at the front of the bridge, but she caught its arm and hauled it towards her, so that its blank face was mere inches from her own. "Heal him," she commanded, and her eyes flicked towards the unconscious body of Adjutant Lux. "If he dies, I will tear that pathetic human brain from your skull!" She pushed the simulant towards Lux and stared up at the viewport again. *I know you're here...* she told herself again. *I know it!*

But as Adra watched, she was unaware that the scorpion-like shape of a Hunter Corvette had already entered the atmosphere and was heading to the surface of the planet.

THIRTEEN

Following Taylor's dramatic success in disabling the Hedalt scout ship, it had been relatively smooth sailing to reach the planet. Instead of focusing on the disruption in the debris field that had been caused by Casey's accidental collision with an unstable piece of space flotsam, the breaking yard had dispatched a search and rescue crew to recover the stricken scout. With all of their attention focused on the rescue, Casey had been able to slip by undetected. Also, thanks to her laser-like focus driven by the guilt from her earlier mistake, she had not collided with a single other item of space junk. In itself this was a feat almost as remarkable as Taylor's near mystical power to disrupt technology from inside the Fabric.

The heavy industrialization of the planet's

surface had been largely concentrated in the northern hemisphere and equatorial regions, leaving the area around where the reserve base had been hidden untouched. Though, as James had noted during Casey's approach, the mines and refineries and general infrastructure on the planet were creeping ever southward. Sooner or later, the Hedalt would have discovered the base.

As it was, Casey had managed to guide them to the surface without being detected. This, and the requirement to skim low over the rocky terrain in order to reach the lava tube undetected, had gone a long way to improving the quirky pilot's dented spirits. But though the cave tunnel leading into the lava tube was actually wider than the one leading to the main Contingency base, the cavern itself was barely a fifth the size.

Several hours had elapsed since Casey had set the Contingency One down next to the two larger transport ships that had remained buried in the cave for centuries. After an initial scan, they were relieved to find the base was operational, including all of the five hundred and fifty stasis chambers. Five hundred of these were flight crew – mostly pilots and tactical and technical specialists – plus fifty fully-qualified captains. Taylor had been concerned that this would mean some of ninety-nine Nimrod-class cruisers back at the main base would need to be commanded by inexperienced or even unqualified crew members, but Sonner had shrugged this off. "We don't need them to be able to pass the captain's exam," she had said, "We just need folk who can keep a calm head under fire, and who know how to shoot back." The other fifty stasis pods contained a variety of support crew for the reserve base; medical staff, engineers, administrators and command-level admin officers.

James had been tasked with overseeing the operation to wake the crew. Due to the fact that the reserve base had been designed to remain inactive until needed, the stasis chambers had been specifically configured for longer-term hibernation. This had meant that the freshly thawed-out reserve crew members were not suffering from anything like the severity of hibernation sickness that Sonner and those on the asteroid base had been compelled to endure. This was fortunate for all concerned, as it meant that the process of loading everyone on-board the two transport ships was already nearing completion. No-one wanted to remain on an enemy-occupied planet for any longer than was necessary.

Taylor, Sonner and Casey had spent the time working on more operational matters. Sonner had commandeered one of the corner offices in the medical center and all of them were standing around a clinically pristine, white circular table, looking over the crew and supplies manifests.

Casey had been working out how best to load each transport ship with the optimal combination of both personnel and key supplies from the base – mainly fuel, ammunition and, at Sonner's behest, coffee – while remaining within the maximum mass limit. Overload the ships and they would burn through their fuel before reaching the main Contingency base, which was something that everyone had agreed would be a bad thing. Taylor and Sonner, meanwhile, were going through the crew manifest and building five-unit crews for the Nimrods, trying to match up the different skill sets and personalities as best they could. But there was one name in particular on the crew manifest that had caught Taylor's attention. He was sure that Sonner must have spotted it too, and was curious as to why she'd not brought it up, but it was a potential problem and it needed discussing. He was about to raise it with Sonner when Casey spoke first.

"Hey, Commander S, I think we might have a serious problem," said Casey, twirling a stylus between her fingers like a drummer showboating at a rock concert. "We can't fit everything we need onto the two transports and the Contingency One and keep within our mass limit."

Sonner glanced up from the data pad on the table and raised an eyebrow, "Really? I thought we'd got the numbers spot on. What's tipping the scales?"

"It's the coffee, I'm afraid," said Casey. She was keeping a straight face, but nothing about the joyful timbre of her voice suggested she was serious, "I'm afraid we're just going to have to leave it here..."

Sonner's eyes flicked across to Taylor, who was clearly struggling not to smile; twisting his face into a grimace as if he was struggling to contain a really bad case of flatulence. Sonner's expression, however, did not waver, and when she spoke she sounded as grave as if she was delivering a prison sentence.

"Not a problem, Casey," said Sonner, looking back at the personnel records on the data pad. "We have plenty of pilots now, so just transfer an amount of coffee equivalent to your mass onto the Contingency One, and you can remain on this base." There was a dramatic pause for effect, before she added, "We'll come back for you once the war is over. Maybe..."

A tiny laugh that was half grunt half squeak escaped Taylor's synthetic lips. This was partly as a result of Sonner's deliciously deadpan repost to Casey, but also because he was reminded of Sonner's earlier theatrical performances during their adventures on the Way Station, before their current mission. Sonner had certainly honed her acting skills since then.

Casey stopped twirling the stylus and frowned, "Aww, Commander S, that hurts," she said, genuinely affronted.

"Pilot, there are only two things in this universe I care about," said Sonner, "Winning this war, and coffee. Not necessarily in that order…"

There was another brief silence and then all three of them burst out laughing. It was a rare moment of pure joy when all of their worries vanished, if only for a few seconds. Humor was a great leveler, Taylor realized in that instant. Laughter shared amongst friends was one of the most genuine of all human experiences.

"Well, I guess I'll just go and measure out the correct quantity of coffee," said Casey, sashaying towards the door of the office, "I'll see you guys in another three hundred years then…"

Taylor raised a hand and waved, "Take care, Casey, catch you on the next one," before Casey swept out of the office and swung left towards the docking section.

"She's really something," said Sonner once Casey had vanished from view. "It was the right call to rescue her, and not just because she's an ace pilot."

Taylor glanced at Sonner and smiled. "Yes, she is. And thanks for saying so."

"It's a shame we don't have another ninety-nine pilots just like her," Sonner went on, slipping back into her more Commanderly persona. "Some of the crew on this base had only just completed the academy crash course at the time they were rushed away from Earth and frozen."

"They'll step up," said Taylor confidently.

Sonner frowned at him, "How can you be so sure?"

"Because they'll have to," said Taylor, and then his eyes fell on the name he'd seen earlier, before Casey's humorous interjection. "Besides, I don't think rookie crews are our biggest problem. Have you seen one of the names on this list?"

Taylor noticed that Sonner's jaw seemed to clench as he mentioned the list. "What name?" she asked, cagily.

Taylor pointed a finger at the name on the data pad and added, "What are we going to do about him?"

Sonner looked at the entry above the tip of Taylor's finger and read the name, "Colonel Chester Collins, Officer Commanding Earth Fleet Reserve Contingency Base (EFRCB)." When she looked up at Taylor, she looked oddly relieved. "Oh, him. What about him?"

Taylor was genuinely surprised at the reaction, partly because it seemed to indicate she had expected Taylor to highlight a different name, but also because she seemed unconcerned about the arrival of an officer with more seniority than she had.

"'Oh, him'?" Taylor repeated. "Who were you thinking I meant?"

"Never mind that," Sonner hit back, folding her arms, "what's your point about Collins?"

"Seriously, you don't see this as a potential problem?" Taylor asked, not even trying to hide his dismay at how casually Sonner had brushed it off. "He's a Colonel, he outranks you!"

"Plenty of people in Earth Fleet outranked me, Captain," said Sonner. She knew what Taylor was eluding to, but the fact he hadn't just come out and said it annoyed her, and made her want to be even more difficult than usual.

"Yes, but all of them are dead," replied Taylor, sticking to his guns. He wasn't letting Sonner just casually brush this under the rug. Then he tapped his finger on the name again. "This guy is not."

"Look, Taylor, I'm just a cranky, forty-something Earth Fleet engineer. I fix things and I box the ears of other engineers to make sure they fix things. I was never supposed to be the one leading this crazy war."

"Yet here you are, doing just that," Taylor replied, and then with sincerity added, "and not only that, but you're doing it well." This caused Sonner's eyes to soften a little. "You can't be willing to just give up command to whoever this guy is?"

111

Taylor had finally got to the point, and now Sonner opened up too. "Of course I don't want to hand over the Contingency to Collins, but it doesn't matter what I want. He's a Colonel and I'm a Commander and that's all there is to it."

Taylor shook his head, "No way, I don't accept that. We haven't got this far playing by the rules. You should have killed me when you first encountered me, but you didn't. You broke the rules then and we've been making the rule book up ever since. That's the only reason any of these people are alive." Then he leaned in a fraction closer to her, locking his silver eyes onto hers. "You're the only reason any of these people are alive."

Sonner sighed and then rested her palms on the table, bring their heads closer together, "Most of that is true, Captain." Then she met his eyes. "But you know damn well we'd be dead if it wasn't for you, too. And Casey. We've done this together."

"And we need to see it through, together," replied Taylor with a firmness and gravitas she'd rarely heard from him. He held his finger on the name and the service record of Colonel Chester Collins filled the screen of the data pad. Taylor scanned the entry, assimilating the information far more quickly than Sonner's human eyes could. "This guy is a bureaucrat. A manager. He was put here to ensure the base ran smoothly, not to command forces into battle."

"We don't know what's he's like," said Sonner, tiring of the conversation. There were more pressing matters to deal with. "He could be just what we need to plan our attack." Taylor looked at her like she was crazy, which only made Sonner more irritated, "Look, Captain, let's just worry about getting everyone back to the Contingency base first. This Colonel Collins has only just thawed out and will barely be able to string a coherent sentence together for at least another day. So let's park this conversation for another time, okay?"

Taylor sighed and then massaged his non-existent stubble, "Okay. For now."

Sonner nodded. "Good. Besides, he could be a great guy. A great leader."

"And what if he's not?" wondered Taylor, folding his arms. He was still smarting from the exchange and was like a dog with a bone.

Sonner continued to peer into Taylor's silver eyes, which held her attention like a magnet. He wasn't just shooting the breeze; she could tell that this was something that troubled him deeply and, if she was honest, it was troubling her too. She didn't know this Colonel, and whether he was a capable officer or not, she didn't want to give up command to him, or anyone else. She had been frank with Taylor earlier when she'd described herself as just a 'cranky, forty-something Earth Fleet engineer.' She would have been the first to admit that she should be the last to lead the Contingency War, but fate hadn't given her a chance to say no. And now she had come too far not to see it through to the end. "If he's a grade-A asshole then we cross that airlock when we come to it, okay?"

Taylor nodded and was about to reply when James burst through the door, red faced and out of breath.

"What the hell, Lieutenant, haven't you heard of knocking?" snapped Sonner.

"Sorry Commander, but we've detected another ship entering the system," panted James, almost collapsing onto the table and spitting the words out so quickly they practically merged into one.

Sonner and Taylor glanced at each other and then darted for the door. "Get back to the Contingency One," Taylor called out to James, "We hooked its scanners up to the hidden antenna on the surface. It will be quicker than trying to access and figure out the systems on the base."

James nodded and together then ran along the corridor, past the disheveled forms of Earth Fleet crew that had recently been brought out of stasis, whose eyes followed them fearfully, and in through the lowered rear cargo ramp of the

Corvette. Taylor made it to the bridge first by virtue of his untiring simulant body and rushed to the mission operations console.

Casey was at her station with her purple canvas shoes up on the pilot's console, and Taylor's sudden charge through the door almost made her fall off the chair. "Captain, what's going on?"

"There's another ship coming in," said Taylor, quickly accessing the surface antenna and pulling in the sensor data. Casey jolted out of the chair and ran to his side, and soon the scan data flowed onto the console screen. Taylor was able to assimilate it all before the two Sonners finally arrived.

"What is it, Captain?" asked Sarah Sonner, holding her sides. "Is it the frigate?"

"No," replied Taylor, double-checking the data to be sure, "it's another Corvette-class cruiser, like this one, and it's heading towards the breaking yard."

Sonner relaxed back against the wall and let out an audible sigh of relief. "Damn it, James, you made me run all this way for nothing. And you know how much I hate running."

Then Taylor realized something, and he spun the chair around to face Commander Sonner, "It's a Hunter Corvette!" he exclaimed, suddenly excited, "They're probably decommissioning it, which means the Hunter simulants are probably still on board."

Sonner pushed away from the wall, "Oh, no, no, no," she said, wagging a finger at him, "I know what you're thinking, and you can get that idea out of your lab-grown brain, right now!"

"Don't forget our deal, Commander," Taylor hit back. "If there's a chance of rescuing one of the others, you owe it to me to try, just like on the Way Station."

"This is hardly a similar situation, Captain!" argued Sonner. "Have you forgotten that there's a sensor perimeter surrounding that breaking yard? And have you also forgotten about the lethal plasma turrets that would turn the Contingency One to smoldering ashes if we got hit?"

"We won't get hit," said Taylor, but then Casey joined in, fearful that Taylor was relying on her piloting skills a little too much.

"Cap, I know you have faith in me, but I have to agree with Commander S," said Casey, hesitantly, but with no less sparkle to her voice. "I can't dodge volleys from that number of turrets for long."

"We won't get hit," Taylor said again, "because I'll do my 'party trick', as Sonner calls it, and shut the perimeter down. Including those turrets." Taylor's comment had the desired effect of stopping Sonner from adding to her string of objections, giving him an opening to finish detailing his proposal. "We launch the transports and send them out hot, making it easy for the breaker's yard to spot them burning hard away from the planet," Taylor went on, growing in confidence. "They will scramble whatever ships they have to intercept, but the transports will be spooled up and ready with pre-calculated jump co-ordinates transferred from the Contingency One. We already calculated the reciprocal course in case we had to jump away quickly, remember?" He paused for a moment to check if Sonner was ready to object again.

The Commander seemed to be chewing the inside of her mouth, but then sniffed loudly and said, with some reluctance, "Go on, Captain."

"The transports then both jump away before the scrambled ships can get within weapons range. Once they're gone, I pop the circuits in the breakers yard, taking down the sensor perimeter and turrets. We go in hard and fast with the Contingency One, grab the prize, and be gone before they realize what hit them."

There was a pregnant pause, and then suddenly Casey start to applaud. "That's a great plan, Cap," she said brightly, "and it might even work!"

"I can make sure the transports have the jump calculations programmed in," said James, adding to the chorus of support, "and the new transceivers are already installed and working, so they'll have no problem jumping the threads undetected."

"It'll work," said Taylor, resolutely looking

Sonner dead in the eyes.

Commander Sonner blew out her cheeks and shook her head, "I can't believe I'm saying this, but it's a solid plan. Hell, let's give it a shot."

Casey and James looked at each other and smiled, as if they were kids whose mom had just said they could go to the mall, but Taylor remained serious and somber. "Thank you, Commander. I mean it."

"Don't thank me yet, Captain," Sonner answered, "because if you get me killed, I'm having you and Casey turned into coffee machines."

FOURTEEN

Provost Adra stared out through the floor-to-ceiling glass walls of the cube-shaped office that presided over the center of the reclamation facility, patiently observing a swarm of repair drones buzzing around her stricken War Frigate. The ship had been recovered to the safety and protection of reclamation facility Cygnus G7-530 by the Warden of the operation; a fidgety male bureaucrat called Holx. He had dispatched tugs and a repair ship the instant Adra's ailing frigate had been detected, and the massive ship was now attached to the dock in the first quadrant. Each quadrant of the facility was able to process a ship from start to finish, and was typically occupied by vessels that were awaiting dissection, rather than repair. The mighty War Frigate was therefore a highly unusual sight. The dock was also where any remaining crew as well as valuable internal equipment was offloaded, before the ship made its way through the stages of surgical processing to cut away anything of value.

Like the remote Way Stations, which were sanctuaries for the those who didn't want to be found and those without great ambition, the reclamation facility was another posting for those who preferred to keep a healthy distance from the core systems of the empire. Nevertheless, Holx had impressed – or at least not yet offended – Provost Adra through his quick and intelligent response to her arrival, and had so far acted respectfully and appropriately towards her. In short, this meant he had wisely not asked her any probing questions. And he had also made himself scarce by offering Adra the use of his office, perched high above the labyrinth of conduits and interlinked sections that made up the facility's four operational quadrants. The elevation, and the transparent walls, meant that the Warden could more easily monitor everything that went on below. And it was also an efficient, if slightly oppressive, way to motivate the workers, who knew they were being watched at all times.

Adjutant Lux remained by Provost Adra's side, choosing to stand despite Adra having given him permission to sit down. The simulant on the frigate had succeeded in keeping him alive for long enough to reach the installation's medical facility, but it had quickly become obvious that Lux's injuries were more than skin deep. The medical staff had treated him as best they could, but they had neither the equipment nor the medical expertise to attend to him fully. Adra had also not escaped the debilitating consequences of the double jump unscathed, but her levels of resilience were ranked amongst the highest of any Hedalt officer in the entire empire, and as such she had already regained much of her strength. This had in part been helped by the fact that Adra found Holx's office to be an oasis of calm compared to the constant rumble of white noise that assaulted her senses on the frigate. Combined with the near-hypnotic sight of hundreds of automated repair drones performing an intricate and synchronized ballet of maneuvers outside, Adra had felt as close to being at peace as she could remember for a long time.

"Provost Adra, there is another ship docking," said Lux with surprise.

Adra turned her head to where Lux had been, but she had been so caught up in her thoughts that she hadn't realized her Adjutant had moved over to the other side of the office. He was propped up against the transparent wall, peering down at the reclamation dock in quadrant four.

Adra walked over to Lux and followed the line of his gaze, quickly spotting the scorpion-shaped craft as it cruised lethargically towards the dock, the starship equivalent of a dead man walking. Adra's jaw tightened; she knew the distinctive shape of the Hunter Corvettes as intricately as she knew the curves and lines of her own face.

"They should not be reclaiming the Hunters," said Lux. His voice was tinged with sadness, but his hands clenched into fists as he said the words. "If more of them had remained operational then we would have discovered this human threat sooner."

Lux's statement was bold considering he was making it in the presence of his Provost. Normally, an adjutant would not presume to state an opinion so brazenly, for risk of it conflicting with the views of his or her commander. Adra should have cut him back down to size, but she appreciated that Lux had spoken the words with genuine feeling and outrage; an outrage she shared. As the one who had devised the Hunter Fleet programme, no-one was more angry than Adra to see one of her ships sent to die in a place like this.

"Warfare Command has believed humans to be extinct for decades," said Adra coolly, though the subject was too raw for her to hide her emotions completely. "The Hunter Fleet once numbered in the thousands. Now it is all but extinct, while the humans live on."

"Not for long, Provost," said Lux, making no attempt to restrain the anger that colored his words. "We will find this rogue ship and force them to tell us where the humans are hiding."

Despite herself, Adra felt a swell of pride for her Adjutant. Few ever gained Adra's trust or respect, and considering Lux's shaky beginnings, she had thought it more likely that she would have killed him than considered him an ally. Yet here he stood, filled with the very same sense of purpose that had fueled her every thought and action since discovering the true nature of the anomalous signal inside the CoreNet.

Adra removed a small data pad from the pocket of her long, black coat and requested the registry record of the Corvette from the CoreNet central database. As she waited for the data to process, she watched the Corvette latch on to the airlock of the inner structure; the first stage of its eventual dissection.

The data pad bleeped and Adra read the first line of information. The ship was designated as 'Hunter Corvette GST8R1'. Adra did not need to delve further into the records to learn more about this ship. It was the same Hunter Corvette that had been docked on Way Station G-7J00; the same Corvette that the Casey Valera simulant had been stolen from. Without a full crew, Warfare Command would have had no reason to keep it in service. *A convenient excuse...* Adra thought to herself. But, more significantly, Hunter Corvette GST8R1 was also the very last Hunter Corvette commissioned; she knew this because she had personally been the one to launch it. Its arrival at the reclamation facility confirmed that the Hunter Corvette program – a program that she had been instrumental in creating centuries earlier – was no more, at least in the eyes of Warfare Command. But Adra knew better; she knew that there was still one more Hunter Corvette in the galaxy. Except that this one did not see human beings as its prey; it hunted something else. And it had to be stopped.

The console on the desk of Warden Holx chimed an incoming message. Adra placed the data pad back in her coat pocket and marched to the desk to answer it. "Yes, what is it?" she snarled, irritated by the interruption.

"Apologies, Provost," said the voice of Warden Holx through the communicator. Adra could not see the Warden, but she could hear him nervously rustling the collar of his jacket, as he had done the first time they'd met. "But I wanted to bring something to your attention. There has been an unscheduled launch from the planet's surface."

"Not ours?" said Adra.

"No, Provost, but I believe our sensors must be malfunctioning, as the readings make no sense," Holx went on. Adra realized he was trying to cover his back before he'd even explained what he'd seen, and she was already rapidly losing patience with him.

"Just tell me what the sensor readings show, Warden Holx," snapped Adra. "I am not interested in excuses."

"We detect no transceiver identification, but the hull designs and power signatures read as..." he hesitated again before adding, "well, they read as Earth Fleet transports." His voice cowered as if he expected to be struck across the face for the stupidity of his comment, despite not even being in the same room as Adra. Lux had overheard the conversation and hurried to the desk, stumbling slightly; still weak from the double jump. He looked into Adra's intense green eyes, watching and waiting for her orders.

"Dispatch any ships you have and intercept them immediately," ordered Adra, "and transfer docking release control to my frigate, I will launch at once."

"Yes, Provost, our ships are already en route, but..." Holx hesitated again, and Adra wished she could reach through the communications link and strangle him.

"You are beginning to test my patience, Warden," said Adra, darkly.

The implied threat was not lost on Holx. "There is another ship approaching," he added promptly, but there was fear in his voice now. "We did not see it until it was almost upon us. It used the debris field to mask..."

"What ship?!" Adra cried, slamming her fist on the desk with such intensity that it dented the smooth metal surface.

"A Corvette, Provost. A Hunter Corvette," babbled Holx, "but I read no transceiver signal from it, either. It is like it does not exist."

Adra peered at Lux for a mere fraction of a second and together they ran, barging through the office door with such force that it almost flew off its hinges, and down the spiral staircase to the web of corridors that spread throughout the facility. Lux struggled to keep pace with Adra as they charged towards the dock where her War Frigate was waiting. But then the lights in the corridor suddenly began to emit a high-pitched whine, which grew in intensity to a level that forced Adra and Lux to stop and press their hands to their ears. Then all of the lights blew out simultaneously, showering them with hot splinters, and for a moment they were weightless as the gravity systems failed. But then low-level emergency lights flickered on, casting the corridor in a soft orange hue, and they felt the pull of artificial gravity dragging them back to the deck.

"Emergency life-support generators," said Lux, as his feet again touched the deck plating. "It will only be sufficient to power critical systems."

Adra brushed the still-hot fragments of glass and filaments from her face and neck and then peered out through the windows that ran along both sides of the entire length of the passage. It was not only their corridor that had been affected; every corridor and every section of the reclamation facility had gone dark. She ran further along the passage to a communications console in an attempt to raise Holx for an update, but this too had either been blown out or was receiving no power. She smashed her fist through the screen, crying out with frustration.

"We must get to our ship," she growled at Lux, "there is no time to lose!"

Lux nodded and chased after her, helping her to force open connecting doors that had sealed shut when the power failed. Soon they had reached the docking area where their colossal War Frigate lay waiting for them. Adra rushed in first, startling the five dock workers inside, who all straightened to attention upon seeing a provost and adjutant of Warfare Command. Adra raced past them to the airlock door, but it was closed and no matter how hard Adra pulled on the handle, it would not open.

"Excuse me, Provost," said one of the dock workers, tentatively, "but we have lost power and the dock has been locked down automatically. Until power is restored there is no way to access your ship, or release the docking clamps."

Adra hammered a fist on the airlock door and then advanced on the dock worker, fists still clenched and green eyes burning with rage. The worker cowered from her, raising an arm to shield herself from the blow she expected to land at any moment, but then the entire dock shook. Adra lowered her fist and peered out through the transparent ceiling to see a Hunter Corvette flash past, weaving through the web of conduits with a level of piloting precision that Adra had only seen once before.

"It's the rogue Corvette!" snarled Adra, and then she peered at Lux, who bared his teeth and reached inside his coat for his plasma pistol. "They have come for the simulants on the other Hunter ship!"

"Then we have them, Provost!" Lux responded, arming his pistol, "They will be forced to dock and then we will capture them all!"

Adra also drew her pistol and armed it. "We only need the simulant intact," said Adra, "I can extract the location of the other bases from its cranial unit. The rest can be eliminated."

"Then it ends now!" said Lux, holding his pistol ready.

Adra turned to the female dock worker, who was still cowering before her. "You and your crew; arm yourselves with whatever weapons you can find, and follow me, now."

Adra moved to leave, expecting her command to be obeyed without question, but the dock worker remained and croaked a response, "But, Provost, we are not soldiers, we cannot fight!"

Adra stopped, turned and then shot the dock worker through the heart with a single, precisely aimed shard of plasma. The worker crumpled to the deck, killed instantly by the ferocity and pinpoint accuracy of the blast. Adra lowered her weapon and then addressed the others, who were all staring at the body of their dead co-worker, mouths agape. "I allowed her to die quickly. The next to refuse my command will suffer slowly."

The other dock workers anxiously looked to one another and then hurried around the dock, picking up the sturdiest tools they could find and grasping them in trembling hands. They then followed behind Provost Adra and Adjutant Lux as the two elite military officers marched towards the decommissioned Hunter Corvette, ready to lay their ambush.

FIFTEEN

Overloading a small scout ship or even a few sections of a Way Station was one thing, but the intensity of the pain that Taylor felt while overloading the breaking yard was on a whole other level. For a time he had suffered the Fabric equivalent of a blackout, losing awareness of everything other than his own thoughts. It was similar to going through a jump, except he was only aware of himself and no-one else. After some time – how long he had no idea – the deep space corridor resolved again, and the throbbing pain in his mind and the representation of his body began to subside. For a moment, he couldn't see the breaking yard, but then he realized why – it was in total darkness. His 'party trick' had taken a toll on him, but it had worked, and all he could do in that moment was laugh and smile.

He hadn't intended to take down the entire facility, and had focused his mind specifically on the turrets guarding the sensor perimeter. But the act of overloading these enormously energetic weapons had resulted in a cascade of failures that had rippled through every other part of the breaking yard too. As a result the lights all around the facility had fizzled out like candles in a rain storm.

Contingency One... Taylor thought, picturing the scorpion-like ship in his mind and trying to feel for its unique energy. *Take me back to the Contingency One...* And then he was moving through space and in a near instant he was locked onto the tail of his ship as Casey weaved it towards the structure where its doppelgänger was docked. He ducked instinctively as conduits and corridors flashed past, forgetting that there was no way he could actually collide with them.

"Taylor, you're in danger!" called out the voice of Satomi Rose.

Taylor spun around, but this time he could not see her, "Satomi? Where are you?"

"Focus on my voice," said Satomi, "you're in danger!"

As Taylor listened to her words he began to race through space again, moving so fast that everything became a blur, until he emerged inside a rectangular room with transparent walls and ceiling. Behind him were a series of docking hatches, one of which was occupied, and beyond it Taylor could see the outline of a Corvette-class cruiser.

"She's here, on this facility," said Satomi, and Taylor turned again to follow the voice, this time seeing his former technical specialist in the room with him. "Provost Adra and her Adjutant are here; the Hedalt military officers who have been hunting you."

"What, how could she know we're..." Taylor began, but Satomi took a step towards him, holding up her hands to stop him mid-sentence.

"She can detect your incursions into the Fabric," said Satomi. "And she's found a way to trace you, just as I can," then she corrected herself, "not exactly like I can; for me it's... different. I don't know how she's doing it, but I do know that every time you enter this place from now on, you risk her discovering your location!"

"If that's true, I need to be more careful in the future," said Taylor, then he shuddered at the prospect of what would happen if Adra tracked them back to the main Contingency base. Her frigate alone was powerful enough to decimate the entire base, and everyone on it.

"You need to be more careful *right now*," Satomi continued. She still appeared human to Taylor inside the Fabric, and he recognized the fear in her eyes and the way her forehead wrinkled when she was stressed. "The others on your ship are in danger too; Adra will attack as soon as they set foot on this reclamation facility!"

Suddenly the whole docking section shuddered and Taylor watched as the Contingency One raced overhead and then spiraled down in front of one of the empty docking ports in a maneuver that any World War Two fighter ace would have been envious of. That this was accomplished in the vacuum of space using only thrusters and pure, unmitigated guile was all the more remarkable. Moments later Taylor saw the lights around the docking port flash on, and the door lock start to turn.

"They're shunting power from your ship to the docking port," said Satomi. "Go, quickly, before it's too late! Warn them, Taylor!"

Taylor was torn; he wanted more time with Satomi, time to learn more about where she was and how he could find her, but she was also right; he had to go. "I'll find you again soon," he said, "I'll have to be more cautious from now on, but somehow I'll find you again, and I'll come for you."

Satomi rushed to him and tried to push him back towards the ship, but her hands just melted into his body. And though he could not physically feel her touch, he felt a sensation like pins and needles, spreading out from where her hands had vanished. "Don't worry about that, I'll find you. Now you must warn them. Go!"

The airlock door swung open and Sonner, James and Casey rushed out. James was holding what looked like a portable power generator, which he immediately began hooking up to the adjacent airlock door, which led inside the second Hunter Corvette. The sensation of pins and needles vanished, and Taylor glanced back, hoping for the chance to say goodbye to Satomi, but he knew she had already gone. And now he had to leave too.

Taylor shut his eyes and focused, and in a near instant he was back inside the deep space corridor, standing in front of the starlight door, which shimmered in the blackness like a lighthouse beacon. He ran through it, cutting off his connection to the Fabric and the CoreNet, and returning his consciousness to his simulant body. He hoped he was not too late to warn the others, but soon enough they would all find out.

SIXTEEN

Taylor opened his eyes. He was back in his quarters, lying on his combined bed and regeneration table, which was humming softly as its power systems wound down. There was always a moment of confusion and disorientation after returning to his simulant form after existing inside the Fabric, but this time the fogginess persisted for longer. Then he remembered Satomi's warning and the imminent danger they were in, and jolted bolt upright, body stiff as a board. "Adra! She's here, now!"

He swung his legs over the side of the bed, but as he rose to his feet, his silver eyes darkened and he fell forwards. For a moment, he seemed to lose consciousness and when his eyes focused again his face was pressed to the metal decking. There was no pain, but his head felt light, as if he'd walked into a wall and was still mildly concussed.

He gingerly pushed himself off the deck and into a crouching position, hands planted firmly beside his feet to steady himself. The room was spinning, as if he was drunk, but without the queasiness that usually accompanied such extreme levels of inebriation. *Damn, that last jaunt into the Fabric must have really taken it out of me,* Taylor thought. *This party trick of mine is bad for my health...* He tried to shake himself out of his stupor, knowing that time was short. The others were already outside, and if Adra and her Adjutant arrived and took them by surprise, they could all be killed.

Tentatively, he rose to his full height, managing to fight the disorientation well enough to reach the door, which swung open as he approached. Leaning on the door frame for a second to allow the swirling sensation in his mind to subside he then staggered out into the main central corridor of the ship. And then he heard shots being fired; it was the distinctive whine of a plasma weapon.

"No!" he cried out loud, "I'm too late!" He scrambled along the corridor to the rear cargo bay as quickly as he could manage, before realizing his mistake and turning back. *The airlock, you fool, they're at the airlock!* He ran back towards the junction to the primary airlock, but as he turned the corner he crashed into the wall and tumbled back to the deck. He yelled with frustration and forced himself upright, using the wall for support. His coordination was still all over the place, but he was beginning to regain his senses and was able to continue within a few seconds. More shots rang out along the corridor, except this time he heard the reassuring sound of an Earth Fleet sidearm firing. *Hold on...* Taylor urged, *Just hold on...*

Taylor reached the open airlock hatch and rushed out into the docking section. His fuzzy mind didn't give a thought to his own safety, and he was confronted by the skirmish in full flow. Casey was crouched behind a stack of cargo containers, with a body slung over her shoulders, but its head was turned away and Taylor could not see who it was. James was closest to the hatch, pressed up behind a row of storage lockers, firing semi-blind towards the group of Hedalt at the other end of the room, while Sonner was also behind cover in the center of the foray, laying down suppressing fire. Taylor raised his gaze in the direction of her aim, and his keen simulant eyes were able to pick out four Hedalt in dark blue overalls, wielding what looked like engineering tools. But further back, taking cover behind a mechanized cargo loader, were two Hedalt officers. And despite his still slightly addled mind, Taylor recognized both without any difficulty; it was Adra, the military Provost, and her Adjutant, the soldier she called, Lux.

"Sonner, fall back, now!" Taylor shouted out, his powerful artificial voice carrying over the melee loudly enough to catch Sonner's attention. She dropped fully behind cover and looked at him as if he was crazy.

"That's what we're trying to do, genius!" she shouted back, as a shard of plasma melted the corner of the container next to her head. In his peripheral vision, Taylor saw James lean out and fire, hitting two of the four other Hedalt combatants that were bearing down on Sonner's position. She peeked out, checking the position of the remaining two, and then called out to Taylor again, "Just get everyone else back on the ship!"

The precarious nature of their situation and the imminent and lethal danger had the effect of a bucket of iced water on Taylor's head, clearing his mind of its cotton-ball fuzziness. He sprinted out towards Casey, moving too quickly for even Adra or Lux to get a shot off at him, and crouched at her side.

"Hey there, Cap," said Casey, as if he'd just walked into a bar on a Friday night, "What took you so long?"

"How the hell can you be so damn cheerful at a time like this?" said Taylor, almost laughing, but a plasma shard flashed past and slammed into the wall behind them, causing both to flinch and duck tighter behind cover.

"Can you reach my weapon?" asked Casey, suddenly serious, "If you can rain down some shots on the scary armored guys back there, I'll make a run for the ship."

Taylor shuffled lower and then reached underneath Casey's crouching body, careful not to expose himself to any incoming fire. He just managed to reach the weapon attached to her hip with the tips of his fingers, before drawing it out of its holster. "Got it!" he said, grasping it cleanly and checking that it was loaded. "Are you ready?" Casey nodded, "Then make a run for it on my mark. Three... Two... One, go!"

Taylor sprung up first and aimed at the two military figures in the distance, thanking his simulant body for its laser-precise steadiness, before opening fire. At virtually the same moment, Casey shot up and ran for the airlock hatch, calling to James to follow her. Taylor glanced back seeing that both had made it safely inside, and then continued to aim shots down the long room, successfully keeping the two soldiers in black armored uniforms suppressed. But then he saw the other two Hedalt in blue overalls round on Sonner, and he adjusted his aim, but it was too late; Sonner had already jumped up and was blocking his line of fire. He tracked the closest Hedalt with the barrel of his weapon, but despite his simulant frame giving him a steady hand, he still wasn't confident that he could get a shot off without risking hitting Sonner. But to his surprise and relief, he didn't need to. In a flash, Sonner had stripped the long silver bar from the first Hedalt's grasp, slamming his body into the containers as she did so, before using the stolen weapon to club the second one over the head, knocking it out as cleanly as a general anesthetic. She then kneed the first Hedalt in the gut and swung an uppercut that connected with its jaw with an audible, organic crunch. She was back behind cover again before the Hedalt had even hit the deck.

Sonner saw Taylor gawping – a mix of incredulity and admiration – and she again stared at him like he was crazy. "Are you taking a nap, Captain?" she bellowed at him, as he stood there with a stupefied look on his face, "Get the hell out of here!"

Taylor snapped out of his trance and raced back to the Contingency One, but as he did so, Provost Adra stepped out from her cover and began marching towards him, weapon held low. "Surrender now!" Adra called out to him. "You cannot run, simulant, I will destroy your ship before you can jump away. Save your friends and give yourself to me!"

Taylor aimed his weapon as he ran and fired

two shots at Provost Adra, both of which pinged off her dense armor. Then he pressed himself behind the row of lockers where James had been moments earlier and called over to Sonner, who was still taking cover, "Commander, go now, I'll hold her off!" he shouted, before firing again. This time the round cracked Adra's armor and bit into her shoulder, but still she advanced. Sonner made a dash for the airlock door and Adra raised her weapon and fired, striking her on the back of her shoulder. Her body armor absorbed most of the energy, but the impact made her tumble forward and fall heavily inside the airlock door, ricocheting off the metal corridor wall. Taylor backed towards the airlock too, firing again and again, striking Adra in the chest and abdomen and then finally managing to slip a round between her armor plates and into her leg, forcing her to drop to one knee. She cried out, more in frustration than pain, and Taylor used the opportunity to flee.

Plasma shards flashed past and he glanced back to see the second soldier advancing, though his gait was awkward and his aim was wild; unlike Adra, he looked like he had already suffered through an arduous battle. Taylor fired blindly at him and scored a lucky hit to his chest armor; it wasn't enough to penetrate through, but it seemed to wind him and he faltered and dropped to his knees. The opening was sufficient to allow Taylor to dart towards the ship and reach the airlock.

"Simulant!" a voice cried out, and despite the situation, the power and gravitas of the shout compelled Taylor to turn. "I will find you!" Adra bellowed, still on one knee, but eyes fixed on Taylor's silver orbs. "Whether here or inside the CoreNet, there is nowhere you can hide from me. Nowhere you can run!"

"Taylor, what the hell are you doing, shut the hatch!" cried Sonner, struggling to clamber up after her fall. But as she had done when Taylor was in the Fabric and had possessed the simulant frame of one of Adra's crew, the military Provost had riled him.

"We're done running from you!" Taylor shouted back. He was fortunate that his rage was contained only inside his mind; a fully human, emotional Taylor Ray might have charged back out to fight her, and get himself killed in the process. But in his more rational state, he was able to notice something that might otherwise have passed him by. Adra was hurt, and she was also bleeding. She wasn't invulnerable. She could be beaten. And if she could be beaten then so could all the rest from Warfare Command. "Get used to kneeling in front of me, Provost!" he spat, "Your time is coming to an end."

Adra roared and raised her weapon, firing wildly towards the airlock, but Taylor had already ducked back inside, and instead the shards of plasma lashed the walls of the docking corridor, scorching and melting the metal like soft plastic.

"Help me close the hatch!" Sonner cried out. She had clambered behind the heavy door, but was unable to push it shut. Taylor joined her, and with his simulant strength added to Sonner's tired muscles the hatch thudded shut and sealed with a sharp hiss.

Sonner shot a reproving look at Taylor, but did not have the energy to berate him further. Instead, she staggered to the comms panel and opened a ship-wide broadcast, "Casey, we're all on-board, get us the out of here, and make it fast!"

SEVENTEEN

Provost Adra rose to her feet and glanced down at the wound to her leg, which was slowly leaking blood. Holstering her pistol, she shifted the position of the armor plate to expose the wound, and then reached inside her long, black coat and withdrew her knife. Angling the tip of the serrated edge towards the bullet hole she pushed it inside the wound. For several seconds she dug the blade into her own flesh, until eventually a silver projectile was levered out. It fell to the deck in a pool of blood, covered in small clumps of her skin and tissue. Adra kicked the bullet away and then walked over to where one of the dead dock workers lay prone on the floor. Leaning over the body she cleaned the blade on the back of the corpse's dark blue overalls, before returning the weapon to its sheath inside her coat. Finally, she re-adjusted the armor on her thigh to cover the now bloodied and ragged hole, tightening the fasteners to seal the injury tightly underneath the onyx-black plating.

"Provost," groaned Lux, attempting to stand, but barely making it to a low stoop before he had to drop to one knee. The weakness in his body infuriated him. "There is still time to catch them, before they can jump," he added, after catching his breath again.

The main lights flickered on inside the docking section, replacing the orange hue of the lower level emergency illumination with vibrant white light. Adra stared out across the facility and saw that power was slowly returning to every quadrant and section. The familiar beat of a Hunter Corvette's engines powering up then drew her attention back to the dock. She glowered at the rogue Hunter Corvette, knowing that there was no way she could return to her frigate in time to catch them. But first they would need to clear the facility, and until then there was still a chance to stop them.

Adra moved beside Lux, grabbed his arm and hauled him to his feet; she waited a second or two until Lux's own legs and body finally held his weight and then released her grip. Lux remained standing, but only just. "Get back to the frigate," said Adra, glancing back at the scorpion-like ship through the window. "Arm all weapons and prepare to pursue the rogue Hunter Corvette."

"At once, Provost Adra," replied Lux, his voice crackly and hoarse, and he immediately turned towards the exit, as quickly as he could manage without risking falling again.

But Adra did not follow Lux; she was already running in the opposite direction, towards the still open airlock of the second Hunter Corvette. She didn't need her frigate in order to stop them; there was already an arsenal of weapons directly in front of her, if she could reach them in time.

Adra entered the ship and charged down the central corridor of the Corvette, feeling the deck plating vibrate as the ship at the adjacent dock detached. It would still need to navigate out from within the maze of corridors, before it could engage its main ion engines, which gave Adra a window of less than a minute to act. She burst onto the bridge, raced across to the tactical station and slid her hand underneath the counter top of the console. Finding the override switch she held it down and spoke out loud, "Warfare Command control override, Provost Adra." There was a momentary pause, before the console powered up and the main viewport activated. Adra accessed the weapon systems and selected manual control of the dorsal turret. The bridge trembled as the ship containing the rogue simulants and two humans maneuvered above her, still only using its RCS thrusters. Adra locked onto the ship and its image appeared on the main viewport, spiraling and weaving through the web of corridors and sections at improbable speeds, as if it was fixed to invisible rails. But Adra was not looking at the viewport; she was focused on the targeting console, trying to predict their course and next maneuver, all the while manually tracking their progress with the barrel of the dorsal turret. The rogue Corvette cleared the facility and Adra saw its primary ion engines ignite. She would only get one shot.

Adra's focus became almost transcendental, blanking out her anger and the pain that throbbed inside her still bleeding thigh. In an instant she had considered the rogue Hunter Corvette's range; its acceleration curve and trajectory; the weakest sections of its armor, and calculated the tracking speed and angle of the turret in order for the rounds to arrive at the exact moment the enemy ship passed in front of them. To anyone else, it would have been overwhelming, but Adra's mind was as a sharp as the black blade concealed inside her coat, and her instincts were sharper still.

Adra smiled, "You think you've escaped," she spat, fractionally adjusting her aim one final time. "You are wrong." Then she fired a single burst from the dorsal turret and stepped away from the tactical console, watching the glowing projectiles snake off into space. Seconds later she saw micro explosions as the rounds raked across the rear quarter of the rogue Corvette, followed by the star-bright glow of its port ion engine flickering and fizzling to nothing. The tactical console flashed up a damage assessment and Adra read it with satisfaction. They were not crippled, but they would not be able to recover before her superior War Frigate was upon them. Their defeat was inevitable, even if they did not yet realize it, and she drew pleasure from knowing that the scene on their bridge would now be one of terror, rather than elation at their escape.

She turned to leave, but then her attention was drawn to the mission ops console. She already knew the identity of two of the rogue simulants, and she had also glimpsed the face of the unit that had been hauled from the ship by the Casey Valera model. This meant there was only one other high-functioning simulant that they had yet to reclaim – the Technical Specialist, Satomi Rose. That these manufactured beings seemed to care at all about reforming their crew baffled Adra. They were not the people they believed themselves to be. They were not human. Not individuals. Not a crew. Yet, here they were, trying to reassemble a team that had always been as fake as their synthetic bodies. Sentimentality was their greatest weakness, Adra realized, as it was for all humans. If they cared for this other simulant she would use that against them, to fuel their anger and resentment, draw them back out into the open, and force them to make mistakes.

She marched off the bridge, but instead of heading immediately back to the airlock hatch, Adra detoured to the crew quarters. There was something still on the Hunter Corvette that she wanted.

EIGHTEEN

Before Provost Adra had even arrived at the docking section where her War Frigate was stationed, she could already feel the power of its engines shaking the corridors and interconnected structures of the reclamation facility like seismic waves. Behind her, dragged by its ankle, was the disabled simulant frame of Satomi Rose, her arms splayed out behind her and head bobbing limply from side to side. Warden Holx stood by the airlock hatch, watching the military Provost approach. He was not sure whether to be more worried about the assault on his facility, or the surreal and macabre sight of Adra dragging what looked like a dead body behind her.

"Provost Adra, I saw what happened," began Holx, his eyes flitting between the Provost and the body being unceremoniously drawn behind her.

Adra slung the frame of Satomi Rose in front of the airlock hatch like a bounty hunter delivering a wanted criminal, dead rather than alive. An anonymous-looking simulant appeared in the hatch and waited, mannequin-like, staring in her direction, though not directly at her. "Take this to the bridge," commanded Adra, ignoring Holx as if he wasn't even in the room. The simulant reached down, picked up the body of Satomi Rose and disappeared back inside the airlock.

"Provost, my workers have been killed and my facility has been attacked," Holx went on, a little more forcefully this time. That Provost Adra had not even acknowledged his presence, or the events that had just transpired, had made him agitated and angry, and he spoke the words more harshly than was wise.

"You forget yourself, Warden Holx," said Adra, oozing resentment and fixing her intense green eyes onto his. "They are not your workers. This is not your facility. And this is not your concern. You would do well to remember your position."

Holx swallowed hard, realizing his error of judgment, but he still felt the need to press the issue with the Provost. Adra was correct, but it was also true that as Warden, he would be ultimately held accountable for the loss of life and damage to Warfare Command property. "Apologies, Provost, but it is my duty to report this incident to Warfare Command," Holx answered, taking care to deliver these words with the proper level of deference. "There have been deaths, but more than that, two of those who attacked the facility were..." Holx paused, unsure of whether to admit to what he'd seen.

"Were what, Warden Holx?" asked Adra, forcing him to commit.

"Humans, Provost," said Holx, barely believing his own words, "The security feeds came back online shortly before the other systems, and I saw them. I could not believe it!"

Adra's expression did not alter, but internally she cursed this unfortunate turn of events. She still did not want Warfare Command to become aware of the humans or the rogue simulants, until she had destroyed all their hidden bases, or captured them and dragged them before the War Council herself. Since she had created human-simulant hybrids and the Hunter Simulant Program, this was the only way to ensure her status and reputation remained intact. If Warfare Command learned of the threat before Adra had completed her task, she would be dragged back and forced to face tribunal, and potential disgrace. If that happened then she would lose her elite rank. But, more importantly to Adra, she would lose her future privileges to return to Earth to study the history of their race, free from the tiresome responsibilities of warship command.

"Have you reported this discovery yet, Warden Holx?" queried Adra, calmly, giving nothing away.

"Not yet, Provost, I wanted to speak to you first," replied Holx.

"Good," Adra replied, before slashing the flat of her hand into Holx's throat. The attack was so swift and unexpected that Holx was utterly unprepared for it. He dropped to his knees, clutching his crushed windpipe, croaking and gasping for breath. Adra calmly stepped behind him and hooked her arm around his neck, before hauling the Warden back to his feet and then crushing his carotid arteries using all of her formidable physical strength. With no blood flowing to his brain, Holx was unconscious in a matter of seconds. But Adra maintained the hold, squeezing harder and harder, releasing all of her pent up rage and using it to feed her muscles.

Eventually, even Adra's strength failed, and she released her grip, letting the body of Warden Holx drop to the deck. She stared down at the Warden's face for a few moments, looking into the now vacant and bloodshot eyes, but she felt no remorse or sadness. She knew that Holx did not deserve such an inglorious end, but he was simply in the wrong place at the wrong time, and had seen too much to be allowed to live. He was a casualty of war, and he would not be the last.

Adra straightened her uniform and fastened the button on her coat, before passing through the airlock hatch to her War Frigate and sealing it behind her.

NINETEEN

Taylor silenced the wailing damage alerts and then rushed over to the mission ops console, catching the back of James's chair as the ship shuddered and shimmied for a third time since taking the hit.

"I'm going to have to throttle back, Commander S," Casey called out from the pilot's station, "It'll fly itself apart otherwise!" She was wrestling with the controls, fighting them hard just to keep the Corvette steady under the strain of flying with imbalanced engines, on top of the numerous other systems that were down because of the attack.

Commander Sonner glanced at the data on her console and saw that the War Frigate was still closing on their position fast. She pounded her fist on the arm of the chair, "Fly it as hard and as fast as you possibly can, Casey," Sonner called back, "That frigate is gaining on us every second!"

"Aye aye, Commander Sarah Sonner," replied Casey, but this time there was an edginess and unease to her familiar response, rather than Casey's typical brightness and optimism.

Sonner sprang out of the command chair to join James and Taylor at the mission ops station, "Tell me some good news..."

"It's not a good news day, I'm afraid," said Taylor, then he pointed to pertinent data on the row of consoles, "The port ion engine is ruptured; nothing our little army of drones can't fix, but not while the drive is hot."

"Damn it, we can't outburn that frigate with only one engine," said Sonner, rubbing her temple.

"That's not our biggest problem," said Taylor, ominously. Then he pointed to another console screen. "The attack damaged the main energy systems, and the power blip caused the computer to cycle. Our nav calculations were screwed up in the process, which means we have to compute the jump again."

"How long?" said Sonner.

Taylor leaned away from the consoles and met her eyes, "Too long."

Sonner nodded. If they couldn't jump away before the frigate got within range then they needed to improvise a way to stay out of its grasp for long enough to make the calculations.

"I'm stealing computer power from anywhere I can," said James, not taking his eyes off the screens as his hands flashed from one panel to another. "But it will still be a few more minutes."

"We don't have a few minutes," said Taylor.

"Then we'll have to buy you some time," said Sonner, and she stepped back into the center of the bridge, with Taylor sticking by her side. "Casey, how long do you think you can evade that frigate?"

The deck plating shuddered as Casey grappled with the controls again, "If we slow to thrusters only, maybe for a minute, two at the most," said Casey, "but with this thing kicking like a bucking bronco, if I keep the engines hot for much longer, they won't need to bother taking us out."

"Damn it, we can't have come this far only to fail now," cursed Sonner, "I need some genius suggestions, and I need them now."

"What about turning back?" suggested James. "We could try to hide in the debris field."

"Assuming we can get there, it will take away their advantage of speed," said Casey, brightly, "that ugly brute is fast, but it's about as nimble as a dumpster truck."

"No use, I'm afraid;" said Taylor, "even if we could make it back there before they catch us, they'll just incinerate the entire damn debris field, with us in it."

"Okay, so what about using your party trick?" said Sonner, "You go back into the Fabric and overload their engines."

"I could try," answered Taylor, though Sonner could tell there was a 'but' coming, "but Provost Adra knows about my abilities now. She'll assume we'll try that and be ready to purge the signal."

"What happens if she does that?" asked Sonner, growing more frustrated and more desperate.

"Honestly, I don't want to find out," said Taylor, "Likely you'll still be stuck here, but without a Captain Taylor Ray."

Casey glanced over her shoulder at the two command officers, "They'll be on top of us in thirty seconds," she shouted. "Whatever you're gonna do, do it fast!"

Sonner clenched her fists, and peered into Taylor's eyes, "Okay Mr. 'I hate being pessimistic', what's your brilliant solution?"

Taylor's silver eyes brightened a little, and then he said, "We surrender."

Sonner was so taken aback that she actually laughed in his face, before the gravity of the situation restored her stoicism, "I wish I hadn't asked," she said, shaking her head.

Taylor noticed that Casey and James were now looking at him too, both wide eyed. "I don't mean actually surrender," he said, eager to placate his audience before they turned on him. "We stop, blow out some coolant, make a show of being in a far worse state than we actually are. Then we fly the white flag, get this Provost Adra on the viewport and let her enjoy her moment of glory. Let her gloat, let her threaten us, let her think she has us."

"And then when the clock runs down on the jump computer, we vanish before her very eyes! Got it!" said Sonner. Then she smiled, "Whatever they stuck in that cranial unit of yours, I'm glad it's still working."

"I wish you wouldn't call it that," said Taylor, scowling at her, "and I know it's a gamble, but it's the best chance we've got."

Sonner dashed to Casey's side, "You heard the Captain, make us look like we're in trouble."

"I'm doing a pretty good job of that already, Commander S!" laughed Casey, somehow still managing to see the bright side, "But sure; one floundering fish act, coming right up!" Casey cut power to the one functioning ion engine and pulsed the thrusters, sending them into a multi-axis spin, before steadily bring the Contingency One back under control and venting some coolant for added effect.

Sonner stepped into the center of the bridge and stood in front of the command chair, and Taylor followed, standing just behind her and to her right. She straightened her uniform and ran her fingers through her shoulder-length chestnut hair, which only reminded her of how badly it needed brushing and washing. Then she glanced at Taylor, "How do I look?"

Taylor's eyes widened slightly, like a startled rabbit. He was stuck between giving an honest answer, or attempting a convincing white lie. He opened his mouth to speak, but Sonner had already changed her mind.

"On second thoughts, zip it, Captain, I'd rather not know." Taylor closed his mouth and glanced sheepishly at Casey who, as he'd predicted, was peeking over her shoulder and smirking at him. Taylor didn't mind; he knew he'd just been let off the hook.

"Send a message to the Hedalt frigate," said Sonner, straightening up and pressing her hands together at the small of her back. Taylor was reminded again of just how tall she was when not slouching. "Tell them we wish to discuss the terms of our surrender."

Taylor's cat-like hearing picked up James's dry, hard swallow. He punched a few controls on his console and then spun his chair around to face the viewport. "Message sent, Commander. Three minutes until jump calculations are complete."

"Keep the jump engines spooled up, Casey," said Sonner, as the comm system bleeped cheerfully in the background, sounding like the ring on an ancient cell phone. "Let's be ready."

"Aye aye, Commander Sarah Sonner," Casey replied, though her cheery response tailed off towards the end as she caught sight the massive War Frigate swooping down on them like a ravenous bird of prey.

"I hope this crazy plan of yours works..." said Sonner under her breath so that only Taylor could hear.

"The valiant never taste of death but once," said Taylor, also keeping his voice low, but still delivering the line in the most thespian-like way he could manage.

Sonner raised an eyebrow and glanced back at him, "I'm afraid I was always more of a fan of murder mysteries and epic fantasy."

"It means we can hold our heads up high, whatever happens," said Taylor. "Or, at least I think that's what it means." Then he frowned and looked at Sonner as if checking that she hadn't suddenly morphed into someone else. "Epic fantasy? Seriously?"

Sonner scowled, but didn't have time to answer, because suddenly the image on the viewport switched to show the face of Provost Adra. The magnified image did nothing to soften the appearance of her steel-gray skin or the burrowing intensity of her jade-green eyes.

"I am Commander Sarah Sonner of Earth Fleet,"

said Sonner, delivering the line with more presence than Taylor imagined he would have done in her shoes.

"There is no Earth Fleet, human," Adra snapped back, "and soon, whatever ships you have managed to hide from us will be gone too. Along with the remains of the human pestilence, and your new simulant pets."

"I wish to discuss the terms of our surrender," Sonner continued, maintaining her composure, despite the savage response from the Provost.

The corner of Adra's mouth curled up almost imperceptibly to create a darkly sinister smile. "Do not insult me, human," she replied, "your ship is not nearly as crippled as you make out." Taylor could hear James's dry swallow again. "Your jump engines are already spooled up, and so the only reason you have not jumped is that you are not yet able to."

Taylor's eyes flicked from the screen to Sonner; remarkably, she didn't flinch, but she also didn't respond. Taylor understood why; there was nothing to say. Their bluff had been called.

"Before I destroy your engines and board your ship, I want you to see something," said Adra, each word cutting into them like a razor. "I want you to see it now, while you still hold out some futile hope of escape."

Sonner looked at Taylor, and he could see the

first cracks in her armor were appearing. She was looking to him for another wild or brilliant suggestion; another crazy plan that would somehow pay off. But there was only one option left; he would have to enter the Fabric and attempt to disable the frigate, despite the risk to himself if Adra was ready in wait with the purge. Whatever spark of humanity still remained in the glint of Taylor's silver eyes was enough to communicate his intentions to Sonner.

Taylor took two paces back, trying to mask his departure so as not to raise suspicion, but then the image on the viewport drew back, and Taylor froze. Standing beside Adra were two other figures; one was a faceless simulant of the kind that Taylor had seen on Adra's ship before, but the second was not. The second was the simulant form of Satomi Rose. Taylor stared at her on the viewport, numb to what was going on around him. Then shock quickly turned to fear, followed by desperation, before all these emotions condensed into one defining reaction: anger.

Taylor advanced towards the screen with the foolish notion that he could somehow reach in and pull Satomi away from the cruel grasp of Provost Adra, and for the first time he brought his own image into Adra's line of sight.

"You'd better not harm her!" Taylor spat.

Adra's granite-like stare became even more

hateful, "I will enjoy dissecting your inferior little brain, simulant," she seethed, "almost as much as I will enjoy doing this." Then Adra clasped her hands to either side of Satomi Rose's head and with one swift, brutal action, tore the cranial unit off the simulant frame. The body fell and then Adra held the head up to the viewport, presenting it like a trophy.

"No!" Taylor roared, and then he ran to the viewport, as if it would bring him closer to Satomi. As if in some way he could still help her. Taylor wanted to lash out at Adra, to tell her that he'd stop her, and even that he'd kill her, but his simulant body was numb to the rage he felt, and his rational mind knew that such threats were empty and meaningless. He could not stop Adra now, any more than he could save Satomi Rose.

He glanced across to Casey and saw that the light in her eyes had died. Where she was an almost persistent beacon of joy and life, like a burning star at the center of a solar system, she now looked as blank and soulless as the decapitated head of Satomi Rose.

Provost Adra tossed the head away and the image on the viewport enlarged on her face once again, "Now, human, surrender and you may survive a little longer. Refuse, and I will open your tiny ship to space and watch as you bloat and suffocate. Your simulant pets are all I need to discover the location of your hidden bases, and turn them to ash."

"Go to hell, Hedalt," Sonner spat back. "If we're going down, then we die fighting."

Taylor spun around and looked into Sonner's eyes; where he had buckled, Sonner had held strong, and he knew what she intended to do. It was all they could do now. He dropped into the seat at the tactical console and shunted every remaining joule of energy to the weapon systems.

"Ready to fire on your order, Commander," said Taylor, locking their cannons and turrets onto the enormous hull of the ship that loomed over them like a storm cloud.

Adra snorted, "So be it, human. It will be more satisfying this way."

Suddenly there was a piercing screech, sharp enough to cause Sonner and James to wince, but the noise was not coming from their own systems, it was coming through the audio channel connected to the frigate. Whatever it was had distracted Adra's attention, and caused Adjutant Lux to move briskly to her side. In comparison to the domineering figure of the Provost, Lux looked pale and sickly. But as Lux spoke quietly into Adra's ears, Taylor noticed something else; something he'd not seen before. There was a hint of concern in the Provost's eyes. Whatever this siren indicated, it was not good news for the

Hedalt. And what was not good for Provost Adra, could only be helpful for them.

Taylor glanced down at his console and tapped into the feed from the jump computer. There was just over a minute remaining, and the jump engines were still spooled and ready. *We might get out of this after all!* Taylor thought. *Come on Taylor, glass half full, glass half full...*

Sonner appeared beside Casey and rested a hand on her shoulder, but Casey's own hand was already hovering over the jump initiator.

Less than a minute, come on! Taylor thought, urging the computer to work faster.

Then without so much as a word or even a scornful look back at them, Provost Adra turned away from the viewport and the image switched back to the external view of the War Frigate. Taylor could hardly believe his eyes. "They cut the transmission!"

"Casey, how long before we can jump?" said Sonner, breathlessly.

"Twenty seconds," said Casey. Her hand was now barely a few millimeters above the jump initiator, yet as steady as a surgeon's thanks to her unflappable simulant frame. "Jump engines are primed."

"Any indication they are about to fire?" asked Sonner, turning to Taylor. The urgency in her voice was almost unbearable.

Taylor scanned his panel, "No, their weapons are powering down, and..." he stopped mid-sentence as the massive ship on the viewport suddenly turned away from them and ignited its ion engines. His next words sounded unreal, even though they were the truth, "and they're leaving!"

"What the hell is going on?" said Sonner, "They had us. They had us cold."

"That's a question for another time," replied Taylor, almost laughing, "But for now, let's get out of here, before that sadistic lunatic changes her mind!"

Casey did laugh and then pressed the jump initiator. "Buckle up, guys!" she shouted, and then started to spin around and around in her chair, crossing one leg over the other and placing her hands behind her head.

"Jumping in five...

...F o u r

...T h r e e

. . . T   w   o

. . . O   n   e

TWENTY

Provost Adra turned her back to the viewport, severing the communications link to the rogue Hunter Corvette. Her appearance suggested calm and control, but this was merely a well-practiced façade. Under the surface she was ready to tear the bridge apart with her bare hands. A Priority One command had to be obeyed. Without question. Without delay. Not to do so would at best lead to her incarceration and at worst to her execution. And Adra knew to always expect the worst.

"Acknowledge the Priority One and jump to the specified co-ordinates," Adra ordered. She glanced back at the diminutive Corvette on the viewport, cowering helplessly beneath the shadow of her frigate. If she could not have it, she wanted it out of her sight. "And get us out of range of that ship."

Adjutant Lux hesitated, at once stunned by Adra's order, but also aware of the consequences should they not answer the Priority One. "Yes, Provost Adra," he answered, before jolting the primary pilot simulant on the shoulder to execute the command. But instead of turning back to his station, he peered up at Adra, willing her to give him another order. He could not believe that she would simply let them go.

Adra did not meet Lux's eyes. Instead, she remained perfectly still, composed and centered, burying her more violent and wrathful feelings deeper beneath her steel-grey skin. But not far enough to lose touch with them completely; she did not want to let them go. There would come a time when she would allow all of her rage to be unleashed, without restraint. But now was not that time. For now, she had no choice but to release the rogue Hunter Corvette from beneath her talons.

As she watched her prey shrink ever smaller on the viewport, she realized the anger she felt was as much directed towards Warfare Command as it was to the rogue ship and crew. Ironically, the Priority One was almost certainly a trivial matter. Just a petty racketeer skirmish or a raid on an insignificant outpost; Adra's frigate simply had the misfortune of being closest. But the severity of the crime was irrelevant. Warfare Command dealt with all lawless acts with the same extreme prejudice, no matter whether it was the theft of a piece of fruit or an entire cargo ship full of fuel. As such, every racketeer raid, no matter how small, was a Priority One. Adra had believed in this policy without question, until now.

One thing Adra had never believed in was fate or destiny or any kind of divine power. The rule of the Masters had taught her that the universe gave you nothing. For millennia the Hedaltus race had served the Masters, who had engineered and then taken her species from Earth. And not once during the millennia that had elapsed since that act had chance ever intervened to set them free. Adra, along with the strongest of the other Hedalt, had fought to overthrow them. No omnipotent being had granted their freedom. It was not fate or luck, but resolve and might that had given them victory. Yet now, on the brink of uncovering the shadowy new threat from the humans, it seemed the fates had indeed conspired against her.

"Provost, we can still destroy them now, or cripple their ship," urged Lux, finally losing his battle to remain silent. He risked Adra's wrath by challenging her openly, but he was desperate to comprehend her actions.

"You have your orders, Adjutant Lux," said Adra. Her voice was cool and controlled, but she was dangerously close to the tipping point, and no matter how much she shared Lux's obvious frustration, she was in no mood to be questioned.

"But we have them!" cried Lux.

"We have nothing!" snapped Adra, advancing on him. "That is just one ship. One crew!" She grabbed Lux by his chest plate and drew him towards her, lifting him to the tips of his boots. "You saw the asteroid base. You saw the two transports leave the planet! If we destroy them here we will never find the others!" Adra began to reach for her knife, feeling the blood lust almost take her, but reason managed to assert a stronger hold on her psyche. Instead, she released Lux and shoved him away. Still weak from the double jump, her Adjutant staggered backwards and dropped to one knee.

"Apologies, Provost," said Lux, feebly, before forcing himself to stand. "I am not myself."

Adra ignored Lux's pleas and instead turned her attention to the headless simulant frame of Satomi Rose, which was still lying on the command deck. Lux's challenge had drawn some of her restrained aggression to the surface and like a static charge it had to be released. She reached down and dug her fingers inside the neck cavity of the simulant, lifting the frame up before letting out a primal roar and hurling the body across the bridge. It rag-dolled across the deck, toppling three simulant bridge crew like ten pins, before finally coming to rest.

"The Taylor Ray simulant is weak!" cried Adra, turning back to Lux, "It believes itself to be human, and like all humans it craves attention. It wants to reform its crew. It still needs the Satomi Rose model to do it. Sentimentality will drive it to enter the CoreNet again to search for another unit, and when it does we will be waiting."

"Of course, Provost," said Lux, fighting with all the strength he had left to straighten so as not to disgrace himself further, "I ask forgiveness. I allowed my emotions to cloud my judgment."

"Patience, Adjutant Lux," said Adra. Her raw, physical outpouring of emotion had helped to clear her head, and this was as close to warmth and encouragement as Lux had ever experienced from her. "We need them to lead us to the location of their primary base – and they will – then we will not only destroy the rogue Corvette and its pitiful crew, but the last remains of humanity too." She paused, glancing again at the rogue Corvette, now no larger than her thumb on the viewport. "So we will let them go. For now."

Lux nodded and turned to make his way back to his station at the front of the bridge, but he only made it four paces, before his knees again buckled. This time, no force of will or strength of effort could compel him to stand. He could feel the life leaking out of him, like water from a broken dam, and he fell forwards, his head slamming hard into the deck. His vision moved in and out of focus, and then he was aware of Adra, kneeling at his side. He tried to speak, to apologize again for his weakness, but no words came out.

"Simulant, attend to him!" he heard Adra shout, and then he was aware of being turned over, of hands sliding underneath his back, and the prick of needles in his skin, but it was all dull and distant. His eyes focused and above him was the face of Provost Adra, stern-looking and hard, but with a new and strange softness to her emerald eyes.

"I am with you," Lux managed, his voice barely more than a garbled croak, "I am... ready for... duty..."

The life left Lux's eyes and his body went limp in Adra's hands. The simulant continued to attend to him, but Adra knew that Lux was already gone. She lowered his body and stood to her full height, staring down into his empty eyes, as blood trickled slowly from his nose and ears.

The jump engines began to build and she knew that within a matter of seconds she would be required to fight whatever waited for her on the other side. Lux's death changed nothing.

"Remove this body from the bridge," she said to the closest simulant, as if she was referring to nothing more than a sack of garbage or an unwanted piece of furniture.

The jump countdown began and Adra clenched

her fists together so tightly that her nails bit deeply into her palms, drawing blood so heavy with bile and hatred that it stung her skin like acid. Then the War Frigate jumped.

TWENTY-ONE

The journey back to the star system containing the Contingency base had given Taylor some time to think and reflect and ultimately dwell on the events that had just occurred. Inevitably, his thoughts were focused on Satomi Rose. Initially, he found himself falling deeper into a black hole of despair, believing that Adra had destroyed any hope of rescuing her, but where his unfeeling simulant frame was in many ways a curse, it also afforded him the ability to analyze circumstances dispassionately. And the more he thought about his encounters with Satomi in the Fabric, the more he felt sure that wherever she was, she had not been on a Corvette-class cruiser. He was certain of that, if nothing else. And if that were the case then the Satomi that Adra had so callously destroyed was not the Satomi he had formed a connection with. She was still out there, somewhere. He knew he was reaching, and that there was no proof of his theory, but he had to believe it was true. *Glass half-full, Taylor, glass half-full...*

Eventually, he had been forced to stop dwelling on the fate of Satomi because they had more immediate concerns, namely how to get two large transport ships through the relatively narrow tunnel that was the only way in or out of the lava tube. But, as usual, Casey had stepped up to the mark.

However, even with the advantage of Casey's remarkable piloting abilities, maneuvering the two transport ships into the lava tube had not been a simple task. The transports just fitted through the cave mouth with barely two meters clearance around the hull, but they were more than twice the length of a Corvette-class cruiser. Even Casey had been unable to navigate them through and into the main cavern without bouncing off the tunnel walls and gouging chunks out of the armor plating. But, even though the transports had emerged looking like they'd been mauled by a starship-sized wolf, they had got through. And as Commander Sonner had pointed out to a slightly dejected-looking Casey Valera, that was all that mattered.

The two transports had docked first, setting down in the second hangar because the primary hangar was already full of Nimrods, while Casey had landed the Contingency One on its usual pad, with her usual delicacy. The engineering teams had worked their magic while the Contingency One was gone; the Nimrods were now ready to launch and, through a heady mixture of skill, guile and sheer dumb luck, they now had the crews to fly them. All that was needed was a battle plan and the Contingency War would be real.

Pain dug in Sonner's shoulder as she pushed herself out of the command chair causing her to scrunch her eyes tightly closed. She slid her hand over the top of her shoulder and gently massaged the area where Provost Adra's plasma shard had impacted. Her body armor had saved her from more serious harm, or even death, but it still felt like there were a dozen needles sticking into her flesh, in addition to a growing number of other aches and pains and general weariness. Despite this, the pain was not enough to dampen her spirits. They had rescued the reserve flight crews, and managed to retrieve yet another member of Taylor's team, Tactical Specialist Blake Meade. And even more remarkably they had somehow all made it back alive.

That was the 'dumb luck' part of the equation. They had used smart tactics combined with Taylor's unique abilities and Casey's superhuman piloting skills to reach the reserve Contingency base undetected, but then they'd risked it all to rescue Blake. It was a gamble that shouldn't have paid off, yet the dice roll had gone in their favor again. They had looked death in the eyes, and even provoked it, and walked away alive. Provost Adra had them; they had been on the gallows with a noose around their necks, ready to drop, and she had just let them walk away. How, why, didn't matter now, but whatever the reason, Sonner was sure it would not be the last they'd seen of Provost Adra.

"Well done, everyone," said Sonner, releasing her shoulder and placing her hands on her hips. It was said with genuine feeling and none of the prickliness that everyone had come to accept as normal from Sonner. So much so that it almost sounded insincere as a result. "We just achieved the impossible, again. Now, we need to do it one more time."

Casey flipped the last of the switches on her pilot's console to power down the engines of the Contingency One and then pirouetted to face her. "No sweat, Commander S," she replied, purple canvas shoes waggling like flippers, "we're all experts at the impossible now!"

Taylor shut down his console and walked up to Sonner. "Impossible were our chances of escaping from Provost Adra, yet somehow we're still here."

"I've been wondering about that too," said

Sonner, "but we may never know why, and frankly I don't care. We made it, that's all that matters." Then she winced and grabbed the back of her shoulder again. "It was hardly a clean getaway, though."

Taylor stepped closer, "Let me take a look at that," he said, reaching out to inspect the wound, but Sonner waved him off.

"Later, I want to meet our guests first, and we also need to fix up our new friend. What did you call him – Drake?"

Casey laughed, and spun around in her chair making 'quacking' noises.

"It's Blake, not Drake," said Taylor, rolling his eyes at Casey, but smiling too. "Though sometimes he can be a bit bird-brained." Casey laughed again, and carried on spinning. "Between you and me, he's not the only one," Taylor added, more quietly so that Casey wouldn't hear, but he hadn't accounted for her enhanced simulant hearing.

"Captain, that hurt!" she called out with faux indignation.

"Anyway, we need to get you fixed up before we try to bring him into the land of the living," Taylor went on, ignoring the complaint from the spinning pilot's chair. And then he quickly added, before Sonner could protest again, "*after* we pay a visit to our new guests..."

"I'll tag along, if you don't mind?" said James,

smiling at Casey's spinning chair and waggling feet. Then he stood up and looked over at his big sister. "I want to meet my new crew!"

"I haven't released you from duty here yet, *Junior* Lieutenant" said Sonner, stressing the word 'Junior'. During their review of the available flight crew from the reserve Contingency base, it had been suggested that James would be better utilized as a mission ops officer on one of the Nimrod crews, which would also mean he'd get a promotion to full Technical Specialist. "But you'll meet them soon enough. Secure your station, and we'll see you out on the deck."

James nodded and then Taylor and Sonner turned to leave, but they had barely taken a pace towards the door before it swung open. Sonner and Taylor instinctively reached down to draw weapons that weren't there, half-expecting Provost Adra to burst in and attack them, despite the sheer absurdity of that possibility. But instead of a two meter tall, armor clad warrior, they were confronted with a considerably shorter, pencil-thin man in an Earth Fleet uniform. He had short silver hair and matching silver beard, which was still neatly trimmed, thanks to centuries spent in metabolic suspension. Taylor and Sonner relaxed their guards and glanced at one another; both recognized the man from the personnel records they had studied on the reserve base. It was

Colonel Chester Collins.

"Is it not still customary to stand to attention when a superior officer enters the bridge?" said Collins, his voice thick with condescension. Taylor grimaced; as first impressions went, the Colonel had not endeared himself. He shot an 'I told you so' look at Sonner, wondering how she was going react, but he didn't need to wait long to find out.

"Is it not customary to request permission to board a vessel that is not under your command?" retorted Sonner, peering at the little man with an 'if looks could kill' intensity.

Casey had stopped spinning in her chair and was transfixed by the exchange, as if she was watching the cliffhanger final episode of her favorite soap opera. James, on the other hand, had made a concerted effort to blend into the background, in the hopes of not being seen.

The Colonel bristled and took a step forward, "Need I remind you that this is an enemy vessel, Commander Sonner," he said, talking to Sonner as if she was an unruly adolescent. "I do not need permission to board an enemy vessel."

For a moment, Taylor thought that Sonner might reach out and strangle the Colonel, but instead she folded her arms tightly across her chest to prevent them from doing him harm. "An enemy vessel?" she said, repeating the words back to him as if he was stupid. "The Contingency One is no more an enemy vessel than the ninety-nine Nimrods on this deck. You wouldn't be here if it weren't for this ship and its crew."

Colonel Collins glanced briefly at Taylor, looking him up and down like an attraction at a Victorian freak show. He then peered beyond him to Casey, who merely responded with a friendly wave.

"I reviewed your mission logs on the journey here, Commander, so I am fully aware of your escapades to date."

Escapades? Taylor thought to himself. *Who the hell says, 'escapades?'.* He was already fostering a healthy dislike for this new Colonel, and he could only imagine the dark thoughts of murder and violence that were probably swirling around Sonner's subconscious.

"If that's your way of saying 'thank you', Colonel, then you're welcome," Sonner replied, and then before Collins could bluster a response, added, "Now was there a reason for the intrusion, because we all still have a lot to do?" She took a step towards the door, but Colonel Collins side-stepped and blocked her path, holding up his hand like a traffic cop.

"No so fast, Commander, this isn't a social call," said Colonel Collins, "and I should think it obvious why I'm here. As the ranking officer, I am taking command of this operation."

"Now wait just a damn minute," said Taylor stepping in-between the Colonel and Sonner, which made the silver-haired man recoil and take a pace back, as if Taylor was a rabid dog snapping at his ankles. "Everything that's happened so far is because of Commander Sonner, and the crew of this 'enemy vessel' as you call it. You'd still be a popsicle on a planet thousands of light years from here if it wasn't for her!"

"And Earth Fleet appreciates what you have all achieved in getting us this far," said Colonel Collins, barely even attempting to sound sincere, "Despite your questionable tactics, and even more questionable choice of crew mates." He looked directly at Taylor as he said this, before returning his eyes to Sonner. "But, now I am in command, as regulations dictate."

"Questionable choice of crew? Are you out of your damn mind?" snapped Sonner, incredulously. She had seemingly forgotten everything she had told Taylor while on the reserve Contingency base about the need to accept the authority of this Colonel. Far from accepting his authority, she looked like she was about to pop him in the mouth.

Collins appeared astonished at Sonner's retort, and angrily jabbed a finger at Taylor. "Not only does your crew include simulant agents that until recently were hunting humans to extinction, you have twice risked the safety of the Contingency by

183

conducting foolhardy and reckless missions to recover two more of them!"

"Hey, one of 'them' is standing right in front of you, Colonel," said Taylor, who also now wanted to pop this man in the mouth, "If it weren't for me and Casey, Sonner would still be the last human alive. Can't you see that we're not your enemies?"

"It is for that reason, and that reason alone, that I have not already had you arrested and impounded," said Colonel Collins. His choice of words was telling. Only people were imprisoned; animals, on the other hand, were impounded. Taylor took another step towards him, but Sonner held out her arm and looked into his silver eyes, shaking her head slowly. "But none of this permits you to continue commanding this operation." His blustering had made his cheeks redden, which contrasted starkly with his white hair and whiskers. "Now, Commander Sonner, you will report to me in the base commander's office in two hours to discuss our handover and next steps. Is that understood?"

Sonner placed her hands into the small of her back and straightened to attention, which only made her tower over the Colonel even more, "Yes, Colonel, I understand," she answered, though it was like she was speaking the words through gritted teeth.

"Good," said Colonel Collins, finally satisfied

that he had asserted his authority. "Two hours then," and he swept off the bridge, leaving them all stunned and lost for words.

It was Taylor that finally broke the silence, "So much for him being a 'great guy' and a 'great leader'..."

Sonner turned to Taylor and sighed, "Fine, I admit it, he's a problem. But he's my problem."

Casey let out a long low whistle, "I believe the correct term is, 'asshole'," she said, before spinning around in her chair again.

TWENTY-TWO

Taylor, Casey and Sonner stood around the bench in the workshop of the Contingency One, staring down at the inactive simulant frame of Blake Meade. Despite her promises, Sonner had not had her injured shoulder attended to by the trained medical staff from the reserve base, muttering something about there being no time, but she had grudgingly allowed Taylor to patch her up instead. That she had refused to stand still for even a full minute, instead continually buzzing around Blake to make the required modifications to his cranial unit, had not made applying first aid an easy task. It also hadn't helped that she had complained bitterly about the need to remove her shirt, and then complained even more about the indignity of standing around in just a tank top.

Taylor had borne her protestations with the patience of a saint, but even his simulant-enhanced tolerance was starting to wear thin.

"Seriously, can you just hold still for five seconds?" complained Taylor as Sonner suddenly leaned over Blake, which meant he'd applied the bandage spray to thin air, instead of her shoulder. The mist from the spray landed on Taylor's sleeve, where it formed a thin blue gel that dried instantly, creating an unpleasant-looking skin over the fabric. Casey looked at it and scrunched up her nose.

Sonner sighed deliberately and elaborately, before straightening up, "How much longer is this going to take?" she asked, glaring at Taylor over her bare shoulder.

Taylor had at least managed to treat the burns from the plasma shard, more due to luck than any medical skill on his part, but he still needed to bandage the area before he could finally dismiss his difficult patient.

"Literally, a few more seconds, if you will just stay where you are," Taylor replied. "Now, hold still, will you?"

"Fine," said Sonner, pressing her hands to her hips, "you have five seconds, Captain," and then she actually started counting down.

Taylor shook his head and quickly applied the bandage spray to Sonner's shoulder, where it formed a flexible, blue skin that stretched along with Sonner's movements. "There, done," he said, "I told you'd I'd be quick. Now put your clothes back on." Casey snorted a laugh, and then Taylor realized his unintentional double entendre.

Sonner grabbed her shirt from the chair by the side of the workbench and pulled it on quickly, still glowering at Taylor. "Did I ever tell you how much you sound like my ex-husband?" she said, and Casey giggled again. She was observing the exchange with a giddy expression on her face, eyes flicking from Taylor to Sonner and back and forth as their little tit-for-tat continued.

"Did I ever mention how I'm not surprised you two got separated?" Taylor hit back. "I never met the guy, but I feel his pain."

"You will soon, if you don't button it, Captain," Sonner replied, ironically while fastening the last few buttons on her shirt. "Now, can we get on with waking up Blane or Shane or Jake, or whatever he's called, please? I have a date with a particularly repugnant Earth Fleet Colonel."

Taylor knew that Sonner remembered Blake's name; she was just getting it wrong to wind him up, but this time he didn't rise to the bait. "We're all waiting on you," he said, with a wry smile. "What's taking you so long?"

Sonner bit her lip and also managed not to rise to the bait. Instead she just turned and leaned over

Blake again, finishing the work she'd started before Taylor had made her stand still. The last part was setting up the DMZ so that Taylor and Blake could co-exist inside a sort of virtual reality. Created by Sonner after they had first recovered Casey from the Way Station, the DMZ was a safe space for their cybernetically modified brains to interface and communicate with each other. It was similar to the deep space corridor that Taylor experienced while he was inside the Fabric and connected to the CoreNet, but it existed independently from it. The idea was that the DMZ would allow Taylor to break the news to Blake about what he really was, so as to soften the blow before he actually 'woke up'.

"Okay, that's everything," said Sonner as she loaded up the DMZ program on the console. Then she hovered her finger over the button to execute it. "So, are we ready to do this? Remember, I can't plug Blake into the DMZ, without first severing the Hedalt's neural control systems. And once I do, there's no going back. He'll be awake, whether he likes it or not."

Casey looked excited, but she was also nervous. This was the first time she'd seen the process, since the last time Sonner had performed it had been for her. "Will he be able to go into the Fabric, like Taylor does?" she asked.

"No, whatever happened when Taylor hit his

head that first time unlocked something I couldn't replicate, in either you or Blake," Sonner replied, "so his party trick is still unique to him, I'm afraid."

"Okay, so I guess we go ahead then, unless you think otherwise, Cap?" said Casey, looking at Taylor, but he appeared lost in his own thoughts.

Something was bothering Taylor, but he couldn't quite put a finger on what it was. Sonner's procedure had worked on Casey, though not without some initial difficulties, and as his thoughts drifted back to those events, Taylor finally remembered something that had been pivotal to Casey accepting her new existence. It was something they didn't yet have for Blake.

"Captain? Is there a problem?" asked Sonner, also noticing that Taylor seemed to be light years away.

"Yes, we're missing something," said Taylor, as it finally dawned on him what they still needed, "We need a uniquely personal item, like Casey's mint." Casey reached up to her neckline and lifted the necklace from underneath her top so they could all be reminded of it. "It was a strong physical connection to a real object that helped Casey switch on to her new reality. We need to find something similar for Blake, before we cut the cord."

Sonner reluctantly conceded the point. "I have a little less than an hour before my meeting with our friendly new Colonel," she began, "do you think you can find something quickly? Otherwise, your defunct crew member here will have to stay where he is."

Taylor shrugged, "Honestly, Blake was like a locked safe when it came to personal matters. He talked big, but said little."

Casey stuffed the necklace back under the neckline of her top and then gently rested a hand on Blake's forehead. "He did talk big, but Blake was soft at heart," she began, with a tenderness and genuine affection that betrayed her true feelings for the gruff Tactical Specialist. "He had a ring that used to belong to his mother. She passed away when he was only a little boy." Then she paused, realizing that she had no way of knowing if these were real memories from the original human hosts or Hedalt lies, designed to help manipulate them. "I don't if that was true or not, it's hard to make sense of it all now, but I was sure the ring existed. And if it did then there should be a copy on this ship, in his quarters, right?"

Taylor and Sonner exchanged glances and the expressions on both of their faces suggested it was worth a shot. "You two see what you can find," said Sonner, "I'll confirm everything is set up here so that Jake is ready to go when you get back."

"Damn it, his name is Blake!" snapped Taylor, but Sonner's twinkling eyes told him that he'd finally fallen into her trap.

"You have ten minutes," Sonner went on, reveling in her little victory. "If you can't find it before then, we'll have to reconvene another time.

"We may not get another chance to do this, depending on how quickly Colonel Asshat moves things forward," said Taylor, with a level of snark that rivalled Sonner. Casey laughed, but Sonner looked unamused.

"You should reign that in, unless you want to be turned into filing cabinets for his office," Sonner answered, managing to retain an impressive level of professional detachment, "You have ten minutes, Captain, you're wasting time."

Taylor nodded. Ten minutes wasn't much time, but he wasn't giving up on Blake yet. After all they had risked in order to rescue him, to have Blake sit out the war on a workbench wouldn't seem right. Besides, they could use his skills; he may have talked big, but when it came to tactical and combat ability, he walked the walk too.

Casey and Taylor hurried out of the workshop and ran to Blake's quarters, but they didn't need more than a minute inside to realize the ring wasn't there. Blake barely had any possessions and everything that was in his quarters was neatly organized, in strict military fashion. But then Taylor had an idea, which had been prompted by Casey's earlier display of affection. He turned to the pilot and said, "We should check your quarters too; perhaps he gave the ring to you?"

Though her cheeks were physically incapable of reddening, Casey still appeared embarrassed, "No, he never gave the ring to me," she said, looking down at her feet, as she scuffed the soles of her purple canvas shoes across the deck. "He only showed it to me once, and told me what it was, which is how I know about it. But then he went all coy and shoved it back into his pocket. I didn't see it again after that."

"The Blake from this ship is different to the one you knew," said Taylor, still believing he was on to something. "Hell, the Blake on this ship was different to the one you knew *and* the one lying on the table in the workshop. But I do know that my Blake cared for you," Casey's head dipped further as he said this, "so it's worth a look."

Casey raised her eyes to meet Taylor's, "Okay, Cap, but I know it's not there. If it was then I would have found it by now."

"The difference is that before, you weren't looking for it," Taylor hit back. He didn't know why, but he knew he was right. It was like a gut feeling, despite not having a gut.

They dashed back out into the corridor before practically bursting into Casey's quarters. "How long do we have?" asked Casey, quickly rummaging through drawers full of different-colored hair bands and clips.

"I don't know," said Taylor, scanning his silver simulant eyes over shelves and inside cupboards, "maybe a couple more minutes at most."

More tense seconds passed and still they found nothing other than Casey's flamboyant wardrobe accessories. "It's not here, Cap, I told you so," said Casey, sounding dejected. But then Taylor's eyes were drawn to a vanity mirror on Casey's desk, and his sharp simulant vision spotted what looked like a thin piece of twine hanging over the corner. It was barely visible, and dangling down the back of the mirror. He rushed over to it and unhooked it. Fastened to the end was an ornate silver Celtic knot ring. Taylor looked at it and then offered it to Casey, who took it and held it gingerly between the thumbs and forefingers of both hands. Taylor smiled; he had never seen Casey Valera happier than she was at that moment. He moved to the door and waited for it to slide open, before turning back to meet Casey's eyes and extending a hand, inviting her to join him. "Let's go get him back."

TWENTY-THREE

Taylor entered the DMZ first, so that he would be waiting for Blake once he was plugged in. As before, when he had entered the DMZ to meet Casey, he appeared inside the cargo hold of the Contingency One. The rear ramp was lowered and extended out into deep space. But unlike the ethereal corridor that Taylor usually inhabited, this place was not connected to the Fabric or the CoreNet, and so was safe from Provost Adra's prying eyes.

"Cap, is that you?" said a voice behind him. Taylor turned around to see Blake standing in the middle of the cargo hold with a pained expression on his face, as if he'd just been asked to solve a difficult math problem in his head.

"Yes, Blake it's me," said Taylor, trying to smile,

but nerves twisted it into more of a grimace. As with inside the Fabric, the DMZ replicated the human appearance of the original Taylor Ray, as well as human emotions.

"Why's the cargo bay door open?" Blake continued, pointing through the opening into empty space. "And how the hell're we still breathin'?"

Blake didn't mince his words, and both questions had put Taylor on the spot; it was impossible to answer either without first explaining where they were and why. "Those are two great questions, Blake, but first we need to talk about where we are, and why we're both here," Taylor took a step towards his Tactical Specialist, who took a step back as he did so. He was coiled up tighter than a cobra.

"Is this some kinda trick?" asked Blake, holding up a hand to Taylor to stop him from coming any closer. "Are you an' Casey playin' some dumb game? 'Cause if you are, it ain't funny."

"It's not a game, but this place is sort of a trick," said Taylor. "It only exists in our minds. It's like a computer program where we can talk and share experiences."

"What, ya mean like those virtual datin' sims?" said Blake.

Now it was Taylor's turn to look consternated, "What? No, not like those!" he said, sounding mildly disgusted. "Damn it Blake, will you just shut up and listen to what I'm trying to tell you?"

Oddly, this seemed to relax Blake; as if the shift to Taylor being hacked off at him was a step closer to their normal state of affairs. "Fine, go ahead," he said with a little shrug, and then he muttered to himself, "I'll prob'ly wake up soon anyway. I knew that last shot of bourbon before hittin' the sack was a mistake."

Taylor took a deep breath and let it out, which helped to relax his nerves. In his simulant body, he'd gotten used to not having nerves to calm, and he'd forgotten how much more complicated life was when burdened with physical emotions too. *Okay, here goes nothing...* he said to himself, and then he laid it all out for Blake as succinctly as he could.

"We're inside something called the DMZ," Taylor began. "It's a place we created to help you transition from what you were to what you are."

"Oh yeah? An' what's that, Cap?" asked Blake, nonchalantly shoving his hands into the pockets of his pants. He had evidently assumed that he was just experiencing some sort of alcohol-induced hallucination, and so was just rolling with it.

"Like me, you're actually a simulant," Taylor continued. "We were created by the Hedalt Empire to help hunt down any remnants of human civilization, after the end of the war. A war that

Earth Fleet actually lost. That was over three hundred years ago." He paused to see how this had gone down with Blake.

"Uh huh, sounds great so far," said Blake, taking one hand out of his pocket to casually scratch an itch on his backside. "Can we just skip to the part where I wake up with a hangover?"

Taylor frowned, but saw no choice but to continue. "Your only organic component is a laboratory-grown copy of your original host's brain."

"My original host, huh?" said Blake, looking bored, "Who was that then?"

Taylor's brow scrunched up, marveling at how deliberately dumb Blake could be sometimes. "You, Blake. The original host was Blake Meade."

Blake clicked his fingers and then pointed a finger at Taylor. "Gotcha, Cap. Go on, this is great."

Taylor frowned and massaged his forehead, but ploughed ahead regardless. "The Hedalt added neural interfaces to control our experiences; to create a false reality. They made us believe that Earth had won. They used us to hunt down the humans who escaped or fled, by tricking us into seeing them as Hedalt, or at least a twisted version of them. That's what our DSR missions really were, Blake. We weren't scouting for hidden Hedalt outposts; we were hunting human beings, we just didn't know it. Everything we thought we knew as real, was actually a lie."

Blake let out a long, low whistle, "Damn, this is one vivid-ass dream. I hope I remember it so I can tell Casey in the mornin'!"

Taylor switched to rubbing his chin, actually feeling stubble for a change, rather than the smooth, synthetic skin of his simulant face. Perhaps he should have anticipated that Blake would react this way, and just skipped the DMZ altogether, plunging him directly into reality like being dropped into an ice bath while still fast asleep. He wasn't going to accept Taylor's words, no matter how he tried to explain things. But then he remembered what had happened with Casey in the DMZ, and how he directly entered her mind and memories. Perhaps if words couldn't reach Blake then a roller coaster ride through Taylor's recent experiences would do the trick. Taylor smiled, as he thought of a way to make Blake more compliant.

"You're right, this is just some crazy, lucid dream," said Taylor, holding up his arms in surrender, "but to wake up, I need to show you something first. It's a little wild, but it'll give you something really spectacular to talk to Casey about in the morning!"

Blake shrugged again. "Whatever, Captain Figment-of-my-imagination. It can't be any more messed up than this already is."

Taylor laughed, "Don't speak so soon..." Then he thought back to his first encounter with Sonner on the Contingency base, back to where it all began, and closed his eyes. When he opened them again he was inside the room where Sonner had bound him to the chair, watching the scene unfold as an ethereal spectator. Beside him was Blake, whose indifferent mood of only moments earlier had been replaced by one of deep unease. Surprisingly, Taylor found it unsettling to watch too; he hadn't prepared himself to experience it again, especially considering he was exposed to the full force of human emotions.

"What the hell is this?" said Blake, backing away from Taylor. "Who's that?" he added, pointing to Sarah Sonner, "an' what's that tied to the chair? It looks like you, but what's with the smooth skin an' silver eyes?"

"That is me, Blake," said Taylor, forcing himself to look, but even he found it a struggle not to avert his gaze. In his head, he still saw himself as human, and though he had grown increasingly more comfortable in his new form, sometimes he forgot what he really looked like. This was a harsh reminder – perhaps too harsh – but, maybe it was exactly what Blake needed. "That's the simulant version of me. The real me," he added, looking at Blake, who now had the appearance of a wild animal that had been backed into a corner. But then Blake caught sight of the other two simulant bodies propped up against the wall. They looked like shop mannequins that had been caught in the crossfire of a store robbery. Despite their alien appearance, he knew exactly who they were, and he ran over to Casey and dropped to his knees.

"Casey!" he shouted, but there was no answer. "Casey, can ya hear me?" he cried again, reaching out to grab her shoulders, but his hands just slipped through her body. He recoiled, and scrambled away from her on his hands and knees. "What the hell is this?!" he shouted and then he sprang up and rounded on Sonner, "Hey, lady, what've you done to Casey?" There was no response – the scene just played out, recreated from Taylor's memory. "Hey, I'm talkin' to you!" Blake shouted, but again there was no answer. He went to grab her, but his hands slipped through, the same as they had done with Casey. He balled them into fists and confronted Taylor. "What's goin' on, Cap? Tell me, or I swear I'll beat it outta you!"

"I've already told you, Blake," said Taylor, keeping his cool as best he could. "You wouldn't believe my words, so now I'm showing you. These are my memories. This is when I first became awake, or whatever you want to call it. This is when I saw myself for the first time, the same way you see me in that chair."

"But Casey an' Satomi, that woman killed 'em?" said Blake, still angry.

"Yes, but we were trying to kill her too. You have to understand we were her enemy. We were Hunter simulants, programmed by the Hedalt to kill humans. But I fell and something inside me snapped. I woke up and saw her for what she really was, and she realized I was no longer a threat. She let me go. She's a friend, Blake. She's the one who helped me find you."

"Wait, you're workin' with her? After what she did to Casey an' Satomi?"

"I wouldn't be here without Commander Sarah Sonner. She could have killed me, but she didn't. She could have refused to help me rescue you and Casey, but she didn't."

"Wait, Casey's okay?" The suggestion of her still being alive had the immediate effect of cooling Blake's hot head. But more than that, Taylor could see that he had chipped away at the wall Blake had put between them, enough that what he was telling him and showing him was starting to get through.

"Yes, she's on the ship, waiting," said Taylor, realizing he should have probably mentioned that earlier. "It's not the same Casey you see there," said Taylor, managing to force a quick glance at the two simulants propped up against the wall, despite the sight of them still causing him distress. "And it's not even the same Casey you remember. It was another copy of the Casey simulant from another ship. But it's still Casey, Blake. It's still her."

Blake glanced back at the two bodies, and then back to Taylor; the hard edge had now gone from his eyes. "What about Satomi? Didya manage to get her back too?"

Taylor glanced to Satomi's lifeless simulant body and then looked down, "No, not yet."

Blake sighed and then shook his head. It all sounded crazy, yet for some reason he was starting to believe it was the truth. As much as anything, this was because he knew he hadn't the imagination to concoct something so wild, no matter how much he'd drunk the night before. "And what about me?" he asked, nervously, "If I'm a different Blake to the one you knew then I guess I – or the other me – didn't make it outta this place alive, either?"

"No, you didn't," said Taylor. "You were actually the first to fall."

"Was it a good death?" asked Blake, hopefully. Coming from anyone else the question would have surprised Taylor, but not from Blake.

"Is any death good?" Taylor replied, but he knew what Blake was asking and quickly added, "But if you mean did you go out well, then yes. You went out protecting us all, in a blaze of glory."

"Well, at least that's somethin'." Blake turned back to watch as the woman Taylor had called

Commander Sarah Sonner removed the other Taylor's restraints.

"I can try to show you if you like," said Taylor, "But, I struggle now to remember the things that happened while I was still under the Hedalt's control. Each day the memories become more detached, but if you want, I'll try."

"No, there ain't no point, Cap," said Blake, turning back to face him. "You've dug up enough of the past already, and I ain't in the mood to see more."

"So what now?" asked Taylor.

Blake shrugged, "I guess you wake me up, or whatever it is ya call it," he said, with a resigned air, "and then I'll either be a plastic-faced freak like you, or I'll just be me, with one mother of a hangover."

TWENTY-FOUR

Taylor, Casey and Sonner gathered around the workbench and waited for the simulant form of Blake Meade to wake up for the first time. After the experience with Casey, where she had woken up before Taylor had returned to the workshop, Sonner had delayed 'flipping the switch' until Taylor had a chance to update the others about what had happened in the DMZ. But now they were out of time; Sonner was almost due for her meeting with Colonel Collins, and didn't want to give him an excuse to reprimand her by being late.

Casey had placed the ring into Blake's open palm and then closed his hand around it. It had belonged to a different Blake simulant to the one lying on the table, who had given it to a different Casey than the one in the room, but Taylor didn't believe this mattered. They may have had different experiences to the Blake and Casey from his crew, but in the same way that his feelings for Satomi hadn't altered, he had to believe that the deeply human bond between Casey and Blake would transcend all else.

Blake Meade opened his eyes and sat up. For a few seconds he didn't move, and then he raised his hand and opened his clenched fist. There was total silence in the workshop as Blake slowly tilted his head to look at the ring. *Come on, Blake, say something... Anything!* Taylor urged. The wait was excruciating.

Blake's mouth puckered and then he swung his legs over the side of the bench and looked at each of them in turn, starting with Sonner, then Taylor and ending with Casey, who he shot the faintest suggestion of a smile. Then he stared back down at the ring in his hand and gently flipped it over between his fingers and thumb, as much observing the strange new digits as the ring they held. "Well, I guess the good news is that I don't have a hangover," he said, looking up at Taylor.

Of all the first words he imagined coming out of Blake's mouth, these were not among them, and Taylor was struck dumb. But then Casey laughed, freely and easily, body bent forward to rest her hands on her knees, as if her non-existent stomach muscles were buckling from the strain of laughing.

And then Taylor found himself laughing too.

Sonner looked at them both in utter disbelief, before glancing across to Blake, who was grinning like the proverbial Cheshire cat. "Honestly, I don't know what's madder; the fact that you all find this so funny, or that you somehow convinced me it was a good idea."

"Aw, hell," said Blake, jumping down off the bench and looking at Taylor, "don't tell me she has a rod up her ass too, just like you? One Captain that's stiffer than an Egyptian mummy is bad enough, but two?"

Taylor's eyes widened and he stole a quick sideways glance at Sonner, but to his surprise, she seemed to have taken it quite well.

"It's Commander, actually, Tactical Specialist Meade," Sonner corrected, "and you'd do well to remember that." Then she turned to leave, but something compelled her to look back. "And, for your information, Egyptian mummies are not actually stiff, but extremely fragile."

"You've *got* to be kiddin' me!" said Blake, throwing his hands up, "She's worse than Satomi!"

"I must be out of my mind," said Sonner, shaking her head. Then she looked at Taylor, "I'll leave you three to get re-acquainted, while I pay a visit to our silver-haired friend."

"Aye aye, Commander Sarah Sonner," said Taylor, smiling, as Sonner strolled out of the workshop, muttering under her breath.

"She seems like a barrel of laughs," said Blake, after a few moments.

"There isn't much to laugh about around here, Blake," Taylor replied, "but Commander Sonner is one of the good guys."

"If ya say so, Cap," said Blake, and then he glanced across to Casey and flipped the ring towards her as if he was tossing a coin. "Seems like you lost this..." he said as Casey caught it.

"Actually, Blakey, this one wasn't yours," said Casey, smiling back at him, "And you never actually gave it to me. Not this me, anyway." Then she winked at him, "Until now, that is..."

"Does that mean you two are now engaged?" said Taylor, amazed at how naturally Blake seemed to accept his new reality. His transition had seemed practically instant, without any of the difficulties that he or Casey had encountered.

"No way, I ain't getting' down on one knee for no-one," said Blake, though he was still smiling.

Casey laughed, "That's okay, Blakey, the only reason I'd want someone to get down on one knee for me is to tie my shoelaces."

Blake looked down at her purple canvas shoes and then back at Casey. "Those're new."

"There's a lot around here that's new," Taylor said, feeling the need to interrupt their remarkably natural first encounter so that he could fill in Blake about everything else that had happened. "And there's more we need to tell you, if you're ready."

Blake looked at his new and strangely smooth hands and then shrugged, "Unless ya gotta real body lyin' round here some place, I guess I'm ready. But on one condition."

"Okay, what's your condition?" asked Taylor. He was both intrigued and reluctant to learn what Blake's proviso was.

"I'll listen to all the other crazy stuff you wanna tell me, so long as it's over a drink." Then Blake shoved his hands into the pockets of his new Earth Fleet issue pants. "There has to be somewhere in this place I can get a decent bourbon. Hell, I'd settle for a crappy one!"

"Umm," said Taylor, not knowing how to break the news to him. Fortunately, he didn't have to, because Casey stepped forward and hooked her arm through Blake's.

"I don't know how to tell you this, Blakey," she said, trying her best to sound sincere, but failing miserably. Then she patted Blake's simulant stomach, which was as solid as a heavy-duty punch bag. "But simulants don't eat or drink."

Blake looked like someone who'd just been told their dog had died. "You've gotta be messing with me?!" he cried, and then shot a disgusted look at Taylor. "Why the hell d'ya leave that part out?"

TWENTY-FIVE

Adra's War Frigate emerged from the jump, finally releasing her from the vicious pain that had gripped her mind, and that now bled out into her muscles and bones. She was holding on to the pilots' chairs, clenching so tightly that the metal had twisted under the strain. With Lux gone, she had taken up his position at the front of the bridge for the second of the jumps required to reach the system where racketeers were raiding an asteroid mining operation. It was one of thousands of such mining operations spread throughout the empire, and Adra knew its loss would be no more significant than cutting down a single tree in a forest. Yet this is what had drawn her away from the rogue Hunter Corvette. This was a Priority One.

She glanced down at the Adjutant's console and saw that five ships were in the system; three Hedalt mining ships and two others, neither of which were transmitting identification signals.

Adra prised her hand away from the metal frame and let it fall onto the shoulder of the primary pilot simulant, using its body to support her own. "Intercept the closest racketeer vessel," she ordered. Her voice sounded crackly and strained, as if invisible hands had closed around her throat. The pilot simulant obeyed and the great War Frigate began to accelerate.

Adra tore her other hand away from the metal frame and returned to her command platform. The short walk was excruciating. It felt like every muscle and joint in her body was on fire, and that her head was ready to crack open like an egg. Every screen and flashing console indicator was like a plasma shard to her eyeballs, forcing her to lower the light level on the bridge by thirty percent, but even this barely lessened the pain.

She pointed to a screen in the halo above her head and pulled her hand to her chest, drawing it down in front of her. She had to shield her eyes against the glare with the palm of her hand. "Screen brightness to fifty percent," she said, still squinting through her fingers until the light output reduced to a level she could tolerate. The screen displayed a detailed medical bioscan of her body, highlighting areas of severe neurological trauma. Almost any other Hedalt with trauma this severe would either be dead already or in a coma. But Provost Adra was no ordinary Hedalt. Over the centuries she had survived countless battles, and irrespective of whether the fights were ship-to-ship, hand-to-hand or even political in nature, she had always come out stronger. This battle was no different, she told herself. She would endure whatever pain was required in order to accomplish her mission and keep her status and reputation intact. Her future on Earth depended on it.

She pressed three boxes on the screen, selecting the recommended neurogenesis, neurological and genetic treatments, all of which would first intensify her discomfort, before delivering any improvement. The screen border flashed red, causing her to wince again, and then a message appeared: 'Recommend induced coma for selected treatments. Return to nearest medical facility.' Adra dismissed the message and overrode the warning, adding a powerful stimulant to the cocktail of medications, before initiating the treatment program. She then waved the screen away and drew down another, which displayed a tactical analysis of the ships in the system.

The three mining ships were modified light freighters, and they were unarmed save for their mining lasers. The crew would have been almost entirely simulants, with maybe a single Hedalt to co-ordinate the operation. But Adra knew that neither this individual, nor the unsophisticated simulant crews possessed the ability to employ these lasers in combat. *Easy pickings...* Adra thought. *The preferred target of cowards.*

The two racketeer ships were Earth Fleet Nimrod-class cruisers, likely found dead in space or stolen from a low-security reclamation facility. But their many modifications meant that neither ship bore much of a resemblance to the original design. They were a rung above most racketeer ships in terms of combat capabilities, but still vastly outclassed by Adra's frigate.

"Mining Freighter Alpha has taken damage and lost engine power," came the monotonous voice of a simulant at a tactical station. Normally, simulants would remain silent, but without Lux to relay the tactical situation, Adra had grudgingly enabled their vocal processors. But the anemic sound of their simulated voices just fueled her anger. "The lead racketeer has latched on. The escort is moving to intercept."

Racketeer tactics evolved even more slowly than primordial life, and Adra felt insulted that they would attempt such an obvious move. The escort was not foolish enough to engage a War Frigate head on, unless its captain had a death wish. It was merely an attempt to frustrate and antagonize her, and occupy her attention for long enough that that the lead ship could cut through into the cargo hold, grab whatever it could in short order, and move off safely. But Adra was in no mood for their games.

"Maintain course towards the lead ship," Adra ordered, as a medical simulant entered the bridge and stepped onto the command platform beside her, waiting for her instructions. Adra took off her long black coat, folding it and placing it neatly on the platform, before removing her armored jacket and laying it on top. The medical simulant approached and held out a small tray, containing a single yellow tablet, which Adra took and placed on her tongue. The effect of the stimulant was nearly instantaneous, waking up her senses like a jolt of electricity. She then extended her arm towards the simulant, which administered three injections in rapid succession, two into Adra's veins and the third into the muscle of her upper arm. At first she felt nothing other than the stab of the needles, but then the pain hit her like a battering ram. Her muscles went into spasm and she reached out and latched onto the medical simulant, clutching its shoulders to steel herself against the agony that intensified with each passing second. Her grip tightened harder and harder and the pain continued to swell until she cried out, unable to bear it any longer. Her fingers were now digging so deeply into the simulant's synthetic flesh that they pressed against its metal exoskeleton. But still the flames inside her body grew hotter. Finally, unable to bear it any longer, she ripped her hands away from the simulant, tearing its arms away from its torso, and screaming until there was no air left in her lungs. The medical simulant staggered back, electrical sparks arcing from its exposed sockets, before falling and landing half on and half off the command platform.

For a time Adra saw nothing but blinding light, and was deafened by a pulsating roar in her ears, like a waterfall inside her head. When her eyes focused again, she realized she was on her knees in the center of the command platform, still holding the arms of the medical simulant by her side. There was an alert sounding and she could feel the thud of weapons impacting on the hull. She shook the simulant limbs loose and then stood up, wiping a clear mucus from her nose and from her neck, where it had also seeped from her ears. The pain was still constant, but her frame of reference had changed. Now the needles of fire that stabbed into her body felt like nettle stings compared to what she had just endured.

The bridge shook again as another blast landed on the hull. She looked at the screen, still dangling down on a thin metal arm where she had left it, and saw that the frigate was still heading directly towards the lead racketeer. The ship was attached to the disabled freighter, sucking out its cargo like a leech, while the escort had fallen in behind the frigate. But it was keeping a cautious distance, no doubt wondering why the huge warship appeared to be on a collision course with its own freighter. It still fired constantly, but because of the distance between them, its weapons had been unable to penetrate the frigate's armor.

"Collision with Mining Freighter Alpha in sixty seconds," came the droning voice of the secondary pilot simulant.

Whether it was the relative difference in pain levels or the effect of the volatile concoction of medications she had pumped into her system, Adra was starting to feel strong again. She stepped down from the command platform and marched towards the front of the bridge, pushing the primary pilot simulant from its chair and sitting down in its place. She assumed manual control and carefully adjusted the trajectory of the frigate as well as the angle and position of its hawk-like wings, but she did not reduce her rate of approach.

"Collision imminent," said the secondary pilot simulant with a detached aloofness that made what should have been a dire warning sound like a routine status update.

Adra knew they were still on a collision course; she intended to collide with the racketeer ship. But this was no suicide run. Adra sat back in the stark metal-framed chair and peered up at the viewport as the frigate's wing sliced between the racketeer ship and the freighter with the precision of a samurai decapitating a defeated general. The sudden, explosive decompression pushed the freighter and racketeer ships apart, sending the latter into a frenzied spin, while the freighter lurched off, spilling its remaining cargo of metal ore into space like blood from an opened vein. Seconds later the damaged racketeer ship exploded, casting a bright orange glow across the bridge and stinging Adra's eyes, but she did not blink, or even squint.

Taking the controls again, Adra initiated a hard deceleration, spinning the War Frigate around to face the escort ship, whose pursuit had carried it towards the collision site and exactly where she wanted it to be. The smaller ship had also turned and was desperately trying to alter course to escape, but it was like a race between a single-engine turboprop and a jet fighter. The smaller ship simply did not have the power to save itself.

Adra always enjoyed trying to imagine what was going through the minds of her enemies at the moment the inevitability of their defeat and death became clear. By now the crew of this little racketeer ship would know they could not escape, and would be panicking, and maybe even fighting amongst themselves. The captain would be aware that Warfare Command would offer the chance to surrender, because it preferred to parade criminals and traitors as examples to others who would consider defying their authority. It would soon send a message of surrender to the frigate and then its captain – as other racketeer scum had done before – would arrogantly demand a trial, believing that it would at least save their skins. But Adra had wasted enough time on these parasites already.

She pushed herself out of the pilot's chair and marched back to the command platform, twisting the screen she had lowered earlier to face her. The communications station chimed and the simulant stationed there read out the message from the racketeer ship, exactly as she had expected. *Predictable... Pathetic...* Adra thought as she locked the main plasma cannons on to the vessel. The communications console chimed again, but Adra was not interested in talking. She tapped the screen and fired, before watching on the viewport as the jagged shards of plasma ripped through the racketeer vessel, reducing it to atoms and molten fragments of metal in seconds.

Adra waved the screen away and then picked up her armored jacket and coat from the deck and put them both back on. "Clear up this mess," she said out loud, not directing the command to any simulant in particular, but soon the severed arms of the medical simulant along with its crippled body were being removed from the bridge.

With the Priority One dealt with, Adra was now free to continue her search for the rogue Hunter Corvette and simulants. And though the trail had gone cold, if she was correct about their desire to rescue a Satomi Rose unit, then she knew where to pick up the search.

"Access the CoreNet and map the locations of any remaining Satomi Rose simulants," Adra called out. "Monitor each location for signs of the signal anomaly and alert me at once if any incursion is detected." There was a monosyllabic reply from one of the simulant stations, but Adra paid it no attention and turned to leave, intending to get some rest to allow her battered body to heal. Even she knew there were limits to how much punishment her brain and nervous system could endure. But she could not wait too long before continuing her search, because she also knew that, sooner or later, Warfare Command would order her back to the home world to explain her actions.

She reached the edge of the command platform, before another alert sounded on the bridge, this time from the tactical station. Adra stopped and then stared up at the halo of screens. "Report!" she bellowed.

"Three vessels have entered the system,"

droned the tactical simulant.

"Racketeers?"

"Negative. All are Warfare Command vessels. Transceiver signals identify two Corvus-class cruisers and one War Carrier."

"A War Carrier?" said Adra, with a sudden sense of foreboding. "Show me."

The image on the viewport switched to show the three approaching ships. The Corvus cruisers were powerful, despite their age, and one of the mainstays of the empire's battle armada, but they were still less than half the size of Adra's frigate. The War Carrier, however, was something else entirely. Four times the size of even Adra's goliath vessel, it was Warfare Command's flagship. There was only one War Carrier in operation, and only one with the rank of high provost could command such as vessel. Adra knew immediately that its presence in the system meant only one thing – that her hunt had come to an end.

The communications console chimed and the simulant stationed there read the message out loud. "Message received from War Carrier," the simulant intoned dully. "Message reads: by order of High Provost Kagan, power down and prepare to be boarded."

TWENTY-SIX

Sonner swung open the door and sauntered into the room without knocking. The office that Collins had commandeered would have belonged to the Group Commander of the Contingency base, should he have survived stasis, but the new Colonel already appeared quite at home. He was busy unpacking two storage containers that he'd had shipped across from the transport. Many of the items were personal in nature, such as framed photographs of himself and someone Sonner assumed to be his wife, and others of teenaged children – a boy and a girl. She hadn't even considered that Collins might have had a family, and she felt a sudden sadness and sympathy for the man, knowing that they were all now long-dead.

"Nice photos," said Sonner, standing just inside

the door. This appeared to startle Colonel Collins and he jerked around to look at her, before picking up one of the photos that was lying face up and turning it over so that Sonner couldn't see it anymore.

"It's protocol to knock before entering," grumbled Colonel Collins, hurriedly arranging some of the items on the desk, before closing the lid of the container and facing Sonner. "Protocol is clearly something you've had no need for recently, but if we're to fight this campaign, we need to start operating like a military unit again."

The response immediately put Sonner on edge and any sympathy she'd felt melted away. She'd attempted an ice-breaker, something to perhaps begin their meeting on a more personal level, but Collins had just shut her down and shut her out. It seemed clear that he wasn't interested in her as an advisor or as an equal. He saw her as a threat, and any commander that was unwilling to listen to advise was a danger.

"When you arrived on the Contingency base, what did you see, Colonel?" asked Sonner, keeping her voice level.

Collins frowned. "What do you mean?"

"Were the docking procedures in operation? Was your ship guided to its correct pad? Were your crew met on arrival and the correct safety and unloading procedures applied?"

"Well, yes, everything appeared to be as expected," said Collins, becoming flustered.

"And the fleet of Nimrods, have you managed to inspect them?" Sonner went on.

"Not every one of them, of course," Collins replied, crabbily, "but I spoke to the deck chief who said they have all been made space-worthy and ready for combat."

"And have you reviewed the flight crew rosters and simulator training plans?" Sonner went on, but Collins had already grown tired and frustrated with her questions.

"Do you have a point, Commander?" he snapped.

"My point, Colonel, is that this base is already operating as a unit," Sonner hit back, unable to keep a lid on her own frustrations, "and it was long before you arrived. Yet here you are talking to me like I'm some damn rookie and that everything is a shambles."

Collins straightened and lifted his chin a little, while keeping his narrowed eyes focused on Sonner. She silently cursed herself, knowing she'd again pushed him too hard.

"I understand it must be difficult for you to accept my command," Collins began, though the formal delivery conveyed no suggestion of any emotional empathy for Sonner's position, "and I appreciate all that you have done to get us to this point."

Here's comes the but... Sonner thought.

"But this operation is now under *my* command," Collins continued. "You can either accept my authority or not, but if you do not I will have you relieved." Then he stepped around the deck and stood directly in front of Sonner. "To choose that course of action would, however, show extreme selfishness. There are so few of us left, and we cannot afford to lose an officer with your skillset."

Sonner held her ground, but bit her tongue. Of all the things he could accuse her of, selfishness was one of the more absurd and insulting. She pressed her hands behind her back, which was all she could do to stop herself from strangling him.

"Follow my orders and, against my better judgement, I will permit the simulants you have supposedly awakened..." Collins made the inverted commas gesture with his fingers as he said 'awakened, "...to continue operating the captured enemy Corvette." Sonner was now really struggling to fight the urge to throttle the Colonel. "But *you* are responsible for them. Any suggestion that they could compromise this operation and they will be destroyed, and you will be held accountable."

"You would be dead if it weren't for Captain Ray and the others, Colonel," seethed Sonner, "I would strongly urge you to bear that in mind."

Then before Collins could come back at her, she added, "That being said, I will accept your command, Colonel." This took Collins by surprise, and the suggestion of a smile curled his whiskery lips, but Sonner hadn't finished, "But I will do what needs to be done to ensure the success of the Contingency. This isn't about petty squabbles over rank. This isn't about me or you. It's about life and death and ensuring the human race has both a future and a home."

"I am aware of that, Commander," replied Collins, pressing his shoulders back slightly to puff out his chest, "But so long as we follow the plans that were laid out by the Contingency Council then we will be victorious. Of that I have no doubt whatsoever."

Sonner folded her arms and shook her head. She couldn't believe what she was hearing, "You can't be serious? Your plan is to execute a strategy that was devised over three hundred years ago?"

Sonner's confrontational stance and delivery made Collins bristle again. She might as well have asked, 'Are you a complete moron?' The Colonel backed away behind his desk, as if placing it between them helped to reinforce his superiority and solidify the barrier of understanding that already separated them. "These plans were drawn up by better strategic minds than mine, and certainly far better than yours..." Sonner's eyes widened and her fists clenched, though Collins couldn't see as they were still tucked tightly under her arms, "It would be foolish to think that we could do any better. This is our best chance."

"Those plans are centuries out of date, Colonel," said Sonner, utterly exasperated at the need to explain this to him, "and so are you."

"Commander, I will not warn you again..." Collins began, but Sonner wasn't finished.

"That wasn't meant as an insult, Colonel, merely a fact. In the time that you and I have been in stasis the Hedalt Empire has grown even stronger. Their ships are bigger and more powerful – I know, because I have fought them and barely escaped with my life." Sonner unfolded her arms and held up a clenched fist to Collins, which initially made him flinch. But instead of trying to punch him, Sonner simply began counting off reasons why following a centuries-old battle plan was a terrible idea. "One, we don't know their numbers; two, we don't know the fleet strength at Earth; three, we don't know how many of these frigates they have, or if they have more powerful vessels that we've not yet seen; four, we don't know what orbital defenses they may have..."

"Enough, Commander!" snapped Collins. "We don't have the luxury of time. Having read your reports, it's obvious the enemy knows we are out here. They will be expecting an attack against

Earth and will be preparing their defenses. If we wait, we lose any hope of taking them by surprise and surprise is our best weapon."

"We've already lost the element of surprise..." Sonner argued, trying to interrupt, but Collins was no longer listening.

"We go in fast and hard and take out their defenses before they have a chance to react. We will cripple their forces at Earth and then blockade the planet against further attack. We leave them without the capability to respond. That was and still is the plan."

"It's a *bad* plan, Colonel," Sonner answered. She was more despondent than angry. "And it will get us all killed."

"Another word, Commander Sonner and you will be relieved!" roared Collins. His shouts drew concerned looks from crew members who were moving through the base – Sonner had left the door open – and both of them seemed to notice. Collins drew up his chair and sat down, breathing heavily, his cheeks flushed pink, while Sonner tried to adopt a more relaxed and unconcerned stance. Neither spoke again until the many curious and anxious eyes turned away from the glass walls of the office and the bodies began moving again.

During the pause, Sonner's mind raced out of control. Of all the obstacles they had faced and overcome, she couldn't believe that the greatest threat to the Contingency was from within their own ranks. Collins was proving himself to be every bit the bureaucrat that Taylor had believed him to be. Before the war was lost, they'd managed to get six Admirals and Generals onto the Contingency base, along with dozens of officers with front-line command and strategic planning experience. That chance had determined a pen pusher like Collins to end up in command beggared belief.

"Make your choice, Commander Sonner," said Collins, keeping his voice low, though it was still heavy with resentment. "My original offer stands, but this will be the last time I ask. Accept my command, or I will have these simulants arrested and confined, and the enemy Corvette stripped for parts. Do your duty, or sit out the war in disgrace and face a court martial on Earth. Because I will win this war, Commander, with or without your help."

Sonner knew it was pointless to argue, and she also believed that Collins would follow through with his threat. As much as it pained her to admit it, she had no choice but to do as Collins said. "I accept your conditions, Colonel Collins," said Sonner, smartly. "Will that be all, sir?"

Collins observed her closely for a few seconds, studying her face and looking for any suggestion of deception, but Sonner's eyes remained fixed dead ahead, her lips pressed together and arms firmly by her side. She was giving nothing away. "For now, yes," he said. "You are dismissed."

Sonner turned and marched out of the office, more afraid than she'd been at any moment since coming out of stasis on the Contingency base, completely alone. She knew that a time would come when a hard choice would need to be made. It was a choice she did not want to contemplate, but if it became necessary, she resolved in that moment to act. If it came down to the survival of the human race, or following the orders of an officer who was so far out of his depth that he was already condemned to drown, she would do what had to be done, no matter how terrible the choice, and no matter the personal cost.

TWENTY-SEVEN

The door to the bridge of the War Frigate slid open and Adra stood tall as the party from Warfare Command's flagship entered. First in was High Provost Kagan, the Commandant of Warfare Command, followed by an adjutant Adra did not know. Behind him were four simulant combat guards in an amber-colored armor that shrouded them from head to toe. The simulants advanced and surrounded the command platform, before standing to attention, plasma rifles held ready. If Adra needed any more of an indication that this visit was not a personal call, the surrounding of her command platform by these specialist combat units was all the confirmation she required.

Adra knew better than most the capabilities of the combat simulants, because she had engineered them to serve as Kagan's personal guard. They were not nearly as sophisticated as the high-functioning Hunter simulants, and had no independent thought, but more of their brains had been left intact compared to the regular simulant crews, who were little more than automatons. Adra and Kagan had spent some time together during the creation and field testing of the guard simulants, so they were familiar with one another, but she expected no special dispensation on account of this. If she was to receive any leniency it would be on account of her broader, pivotal role in the creation of human-simulant hybrids. This act alone had allowed Warfare Command to expand its reach across the galaxy. Adra respected Kagan, despite him ultimately being responsible for decommissioning the Hunter Corvette fleet, but she also knew that he was not sentimental or merciful, and not to be crossed.

Adra bowed her head as High Provost Kagan stepped on to the command platform, while his unnamed adjutant remained respectfully on the main deck. "High Provost Kagan, I am honored by this unexpected visit."

"I have heard disturbing reports of your recent actions, Provost Adra," began Kagan, shrugging off her formal greeting. "I desired to hear your motives first-hand. You have been difficult to reach of late." His voice had a melodic quality to it, which seemed at odds with his formidable stature. Kagan stood three inches taller than Adra, who herself was a towering figure, though like his voice, his face was not that of a hard-edged soldier. Were it not for his amber-edged, black armored uniform and the plasma pistol attached to his belt, it would have been difficult to imagine him as a soldier at all. But a soldier he was, capable of exceptional acts of brutality. "I trust that you know why I am here."

"Yes, High Provost," replied Adra. There was no sense in trying to bluff or lie. She had seen what Kagan did to those who disrespected him. He had once executed a Vice Provost for proposing an alternative course of action to the one he had ordered. He had calmly approached Vice Provost Yuleen, a name that Adra had never forgotten, and smashed a forearm into her throat, crushing her windpipe. He'd then removed Yuleen's own knife and impaled it into her skull through the base of her neck. The act of violence in itself had not shocked Adra; to the contrary, she had found it inspiring. Yuleen's execution was a just response to an open act of disobedience, and a perfect example of strength and leadership. But she had no desire to share Yuleen's fate.

"I have been tracking the source of a signal anomaly inside the CoreNet," Adra volunteered. "It is my belief that a Hunter simulant has become severed from our system of controls and is the cause of these incursions. My suspicion is that it was modified by a surviving faction of Earth Fleet. I have been pursuing these suspicions in order to gather evidence of proof, before bringing it to the attention of the Warfare Council." Adra had not lied, at least not outright, though it was a version of the truth that still omitted a great deal, and she knew even this was a risk.

High Provost Kagan listened patiently, all the while remaining fixed on Adra's piercing green eyes. "Humans?" he said after a pause, forming the word as if it were the name of virulent disease. "You have proof of this?"

"Yes, High Provost," Adra answered promptly, "I saw them with my own eyes, but I was then called to respond to this Priority One, before I had an opportunity to submit the report. That is why I am here."

"You actually saw a living human being?" asked Kagan, again speaking the word human as if it were a synonym for excrement. On the main deck, Adra saw Kagan's adjutant shifting position awkwardly in her peripheral vision, clearly caught off guard by Adra's revelation.

"I did, High Provost, I saw two to be precise," replied Adra, "at Reclamation Facility Cygnus G7-530. They have possession of a Hunter Corvette, which they are using to travel without raising suspicion, and I believe there to be more. Perhaps many more."

Kagan's eyes narrowed, but he maintained his vice-like lock on Adra's eyes. Adra, likewise, held his gaze without blinking. The constant thrum of the War Frigate's engines filled the silence and burrowed into Adra's brain like termites. She was still far from her strongest, but she was careful not to show weakness to Kagan. Adra knew the revelation that human beings had survived would shift Kagan's focus, and perhaps offer reason enough to spare her life.

It had been Kagan who had masterminded the extermination of the human race and the conquest of Earth. This was in spite of pleas from the non-military governmental factions for mercy and a pursuit of friendship and diplomacy; cries that were supported by widespread public outcry once the invasion became public knowledge. Many in Hedalt society outside of Warfare Command were appalled at the notion that after millennia under the iron rule of the Masters, they would then become the very thing they had risen up to destroy. But while the shared ancestry of humans and Hedalt inspired millions to call for peace, Kagan, Adra and the ruling Warfare Council found this notion abhorrent. Humans had inherited Earth only because the Hedalt had been removed from it, and in their absence Homo Sapiens had spread like a plague. And like all plagues, they had to be purged. As such, all objections to the war were dismissed outright, and the thousands of organized public protests were quickly and violently quelled. Kagan had orchestrated it all, acting without hesitation or remorse, even as he had ordered the execution or incarceration of hundreds of thousands of dissenters.

"You should have reported this discovery to Warfare Command at once," said Kagan, breaking the silence. His voice, while no less musical, had a waspish edge that had not been present before.

"I should have," replied Adra immediately, "I apologize, High Provost."

Kagan stepped towards Adra, and though she did not flinch, she half expected him to deal with her as he had done Yuleen. But instead Kagan breezed past Adra and stopped at the forward edge of the command platform. For several seconds he just stared out through the viewport at the image of the crippled freighter, which was now being attended to by one of Kagan's two Corvus escorts. Repair drones buzzed around its engines and repaired the gaping hole in its hull that was left open after Adra's frigate had sliced the racketeer ship from it.

"You are to return to the home world at once," Kagan said, with his back still facing Adra. "A tribunal will be arranged to investigate your discoveries and your actions more fully." Then he turned around, "And as for these humans, I will investigate personally. See to it that your records and logs are transferred to my War Carrier."

"Yes, High Provost," said Adra, respectfully, but inside her anger was building once again. She knew that Kagan was setting her up to take the fall for the human situation, so he could save face. He would then pursue and destroy the surviving humans and take the credit, while Adra would be executed for her failures. But there was nothing she could do to alter the course of events that would follow. She could only hope that the other provosts serving on the tribunal would see value in having Adra kept alive.

Kagan marched past Adra, seemingly intent on leaving, but then he stopped, as if remembering something that had slipped his mind, and he turned to face her again. "Where is your adjutant?" he asked, glancing to the station where Lux should have been standing.

"Regrettably, Adjutant Lux died," replied Adra. She had been so caught up with her own fate that she had forgotten that Lux had already met his own. "He suffered acute neural trauma. It happened immediately before I responded to the Priority One, so I have yet to report his loss."

Kagan glanced down to his adjutant and then back to Adra, "That is unfortunate."

Adra could see Kagan's adjutant out of the

corner of her eye, and though she had not said anything, Adra knew from the tightening of the muscles in her cheeks and around her eyes that the news of Lux's demise had hit her hard.

Without another word, Kagan then stepped down off the command platform and headed for the door. The elite guard simulants turned and marched into formation behind him, but Kagan's adjutant remained, only for a second longer, but long enough for her to meet Adra's eyes. It was a look that she had seen many times before, but only on the faces of her enemies. Whoever this was, Lux had clearly meant something to her. And she was blaming Adra for his death.

The door to the bridge eventually closed, leaving Adra alone with only the penetrating thrum of the ship's engines and six simulant crew for company. She waited on the command platform for the shuttle to depart and begin its return journey to the War Carrier, which had blocked out the light from the star and cast her frigate into shadow. She briefly considered destroying the shuttle, killing the High Provost and ending the sequence of events that would inevitably lead to her disgrace or even death. But she knew that even if she succeeded, the War Carrier and its Corvus escorts would pulverize her frigate to atoms within seconds of the shuttle exploding. She did not know the odds of her surviving the tribunal, but those odds were still far greater than making it out of the system alive, under fire from the most powerful ship in the Hedalt armada.

"Set course for the home world," said Adra, once Kagan's shuttle had docked. "Begin jump calculations and inform me the moment they are complete."

The secondary pilot simulant acknowledged the order, but Adra was already on her way down from the command platform. She needed rest. She needed to regain her strength and face the tribunal at the peak of her mental and physical condition, or as close to it as possible. Rest would also help her to regain a stronger mental grip over her temper so she could better contain the rage that was consuming her. If she could face the tribunal free from such emotions, she had a much higher chance of survival.

As the bridge door slid open, one of the many anonymous simulant crew stepped onto the threshold. It was arriving to relieve one of the other simulants so that it could regenerate, but the sudden appearance of a belligerent-looking Provost Adra in its path had muddled it. Adra waited for the simulant to move, but it dithered, trying to decide whether to step back or step through and to the side, or simply turn sideways to allow Adra to pass. Instead it remained in Adra's way, blocking her path and tipping her over the edge. Adra roared ad grabbed the simulant by the neck, before slamming its head into the open door frame, over and over and over again. Before long, its cranial unit split open and its lobotomized human brain was smashed into the frame of the door. Eventually the strength in Adra's arm failed and she tossed the body aside, breathing heavily and squinting her eyes as pain again shot through her head and neck. She allowed her breathing to relax and stepped over the body, treading a trail of crushed brain matter underneath her boots all the way into her personal suite.

TWENTY-EIGHT

The lights inside the combat simulator dimmed and the viewport flashed on, placing them in a fictitious star system with a k-type star that bathed the bridge in warm marmalade tones. Casey Valera was spinning around in the pilot's chair pointing the toes of her purple canvas shoes like a ballerina, while Blake Meade reclined back in his seat at the tactical station, with his head cocked to the side, smiling at her.

"Okay, crew, this may just be just be a simulator, but I expect you to treat it no differently to a real enemy engagement," said Taylor from the command chair. Then he looked across at Casey, still spinning gracefully, seemingly oblivious to what Taylor had said, and added, "That means you too, Casey."

"I am acting no differently than I would if this was a real enemy engagement, Cap," Casey replied, the volume of her voice rising and falling as she continued to spin.

Taylor opened his mouth to argue, but then realized she was telling the truth; this was exactly how Casey normally acted. He noticed that Blake was glancing back at him, grinning, and he couldn't help but smile too. "And how about you? Do you still remember how to shoot straight?" he asked his new Tactical Specialist.

"He can't remember what he never knew in the first place, Cap..." Casey cut in, drawing a wide-eyed stare from Blake.

"Hey, I dunno what your Blake was like, but I can hit a toothpick on a spinnin' asteroid," he bragged.

"That's easy, you just blow up the asteroid..."

Blake shook his head, but he was still smiling, "Damn, you're even more of a wise-ass than I remember."

Casey tipped an imaginary hat towards him and then continued spinning.

"Don't worry 'bout a thing, Cap," Blake said, turning back to face Taylor, "if the comedian over there can line 'em up, I can shoot 'em down." Then he gave a nonchalant shrug of his shoulders and added, "Ain't nothin' to it."

Taylor's console in the command chair bleeped

twice and he checked it, noting that the simulator had added two Corvus-class cruisers to the combat scenario. The engineers were still in the process of updating the simulators with all the more recent Hedalt ship classifications that the Contingency One had encountered while outside of the base, so for the time being all they could do was train against the older Hedalt vessels that were already in the system. But, even though the Corvus-class cruisers were old like the Contingency One, they were also far more powerful, and Taylor recalled how the last simulated battle they'd run against these tank-like ships hadn't ended well.

"Mission operations, what is your analysis of the system?" asked Taylor, looking over to James Sonner, who had volunteered to man the station so they could run the simulation. He was wearing his new Technical Specialist's uniform and flight crew badge, after having formally received a promotion from his sister, despite Collins initially trying to block it on the grounds of favoritism. Sonner had almost punched the Colonel on the nose, but Taylor managed to diffuse the situation by arguing, logically and dispassionately, in favor of the promotion based on James's performance.

"It's just empty space, bar a small asteroid field between us and the approaching cruisers," said James, "possibly the remains of a comet collision with a small planetoid. It could provide useful cover."

"Very good," said Taylor. "Casey, set a course and make sure those enemy cruisers get a good look at where we're going."

"Aye aye, Captain Taylor Ray," chimed Casey, finally stopping spinning and then taking hold of the control column to pilot the ship manually.

Unseen by any of them, Commander Sonner had sneaked onto the simulator and was lurking in the shadows at the rear of the mocked-up bridge, quietly observing. She had come looking for Taylor in order to discuss the outcome of her meeting with Colonel Collins, but was intrigued to see how the new addition to the crew would perform, and how the dynamic of the crew would change now that it was three-quarters complete. She glanced at the simulator control panel in the wall where she was hiding and read the program settings. Taylor had configured the simulator to a high difficultly level, but not the highest. Sonner smiled and, peeking out from her hiding place to check she had still not been discovered, quietly increased the combat skill of the enemy ships to maximum. *Let's see how they handle this...* she thought mischievously.

Casey was burning hard towards the asteroid field, creating the effect of a comet's tail behind the ship, making it simple for the enemy vessels to spot them and know where they were going. As expected the Corvus cruisers adjusted course and also accelerated their approach, trying to cut them off before they reached the relative safety of the asteroid field. Then a tactical alert sounded and Blake scanned it quickly.

"They've launched torpedoes," Blake said, staying calm. "Two at us, and two towards the asteroid field."

"Smart..." remarked Taylor, stroking the non-existent stubble on his chin; a habit he could still not shake. "They want to destroy our cover, but also panic us into making a snap change of plan." He slid forward to the edge of the command chair and looked at Blake. "Can you shoot down the torpedoes?"

"I've already locked the forward turrets onto the torps headin' for us," Blake answered, "but the others are outta range."

"Cap, I need to decelerate now if we're still gunning for the asteroid field," said Casey, but then she put her hand to her mouth, "Oops, sorry, bad choice of words..."

"Decelerate and head into the asteroids as planned, Casey," said Taylor, "I'll trust in your artisan piloting abilities to avoid any debris from the torpedoes."

"Wow, so it's true then..." said Blake, glancing back at Taylor. He was obviously baiting Taylor and waiting for him to ask 'what' so that he could deliver what was no doubt going to be a cutting remark.

"What is?" Taylor obliged.

"That you're just as crazy as the Captain Taylor Ray I knew," said Blake, smiling and looking over at Casey to see if he'd generated the desired reaction from his audience.

Casey smiled back, "No, this one is crazier," she said, shooting a wink in the direction of the command chair.

"Can you two concentrate on the two heavily-armed warships that are trying to kill us, please?" shouted Taylor with outstretched hands that beseeched his Pilot and Tactical Specialist to start taking things more seriously. Though again, he had to question whether things would be any different had this been an actual enemy engagement. From the back of the room, Sonner was leaning against the wall, arms folded comfortably, enjoying watching the drama unfold.

"Aye aye, Captain Taylor Ray," sang Casey again, and then she began a rapid sequence of commands and adjustments to slow the ship to a level where she could maneuver with more agility inside the asteroid field.

"Firin' turrets," said Blake, and then the viewport showed the brightly glowing rounds snake off into space, followed several seconds later by two bright explosions. "Torpedoes destroyed," he added, casually.

"Two detonations detected inside the asteroid field," James called out. "There's rock debris flying around in all directions, with multiple collisions; I don't see how we can navigate inside."

"Oh, we can still navigate inside," said Taylor, sticking to his original plan, but then added, hopefully, "that's right, isn't it, Casey?"

"Sure, Cap!" said Casey without delay. "It sounds like fun. I can't promise we won't get pulverized, though."

"Well, that's encouragin'," quipped Blake.

"Entering the asteroid field...now," added Casey, but then there was a bassy thud and the entire bridge rattled. "Sorry about that one," said Casey, holding a hand up.

Blake shook his head, "Between his crazy plans an' your crazy flyin', it's a wonder you ever managed to rescue me."

"You're welcome, by the way," said Taylor, sarcastically.

Blake didn't answer as his console suddenly lit up with multiple alerts. "The lead cruiser is firin' its plasma cannons into the asteroid field," said Blake. "They're still tryin' to break up the asteroids and have 'em destroy us."

"Casey, take us in deeper, force them to follow," said Taylor, "and keep us out of harm's way." He was now so close to the edge of his seat, if he moved forwards another two inches he would slip off it.

"That's kinda what I'm doing, Cap," said Casey, grappling with the manual controls while peering into her pilot's viewport. The ship's thrusters were working overtime, jinking the nimble vessel in all directions and spinning it on its own axis to avoid flying rocks. Several smaller thuds resonated through the hull.

"Minimal damage," shouted James, who was clearly now fully caught up in the moment, to the point where it no longer mattered that it was a simulation, because to him it felt real.

"Find me an advantage," Taylor ordered James, and then he twisted his chair back to face Blake Meade, "what about the second cruiser?"

"It followed us and is tryin' to match Casey's insane flight path as best it can," said Blake, "but it's takin' a poundin'." Then he quickly adjusted the firing pattern of the turrets, all six of which were in constant operation in an effort to cut through the maelstrom of flying debris. "It's almost in range."

"Casey, how are you at flying backwards?" asked Taylor, excitement building in his voice.

"Same as I am at flying forwards, Cap," said Casey, "flying's flying."

"Get ready to spin us around and pulse the engines to close to cannon range," said Taylor.

Then to Blake he added, "You'll get one shot with the forward cannons, make it count."

"It's always one damn shot," complained Blake, "Why don't any of your crazy plans ever gimme the chance to shoot more than once?"

Taylor smiled; it was good to have Blake back again. From the shadows at the rear of the simulator, Sonner was smiling too.

"Ready..." Taylor cried, "do it!"

Casey pulsed the thrusters, spinning them to face the pursuing cruiser, and then initiatcd a controlled burst from the main ion engines to reduce their relative velocity. With scalpel-sharp precision she then adjusted the angle of the ship's nose to line it up perfectly with where the Corvus cruiser would be once the cannon shells arrived.

"Blakey, fire on my mark," Casey called out, "Three, two, one, fire!"

Blake fired a full burst from the forward cannons on cue, and then everyone watched as the shells cut through space and slammed into the hull of the Corvus cruiser, blowing it apart in a blaze of fire, electrical arcs and twisted metal.

"Great shot, Blake!" shouted Taylor, jumping out of his seat.

"Oh, it was nothing..." said Casey, then she looked at Taylor and again put a hand to her mouth in mock surprise, "Oh, sorry, I though you said, 'Amazing piloting, Casey...'."

"That goes without saying!" Taylor replied, smiling, but then three solid punches to the ship's hull rocked the bridge, forcing Taylor to grab the back of his chair to remain upright.

"Direct hit!" shouted James. "Moderate damage to aft port-side thrusters and main engine nozzles, starboard turrets inoperative."

"Find me that advantage, Mr. Sonner!" Taylor called over. "We need to take out that other cruiser before it turns this asteroid field to rubble."

"I have something, I think," James replied, thought he didn't sound sure.

"You think or you know?" Taylor replied, staggering over to the mission ops console.

James was quiet for a second, "The enemy cruiser is nestled between a cluster of asteroid fragments that appear to contain a highly unstable combination of minerals," he said, peering down at the information on the screens, "If we can hit this cluster then it could cause a chain reaction that would envelop the ship."

"That sounds like an advantage, well done," said Taylor, slapping James on the back, a little too forcefully due to his simulant strength. "Send the coordinates to Blake and Casey." Taylor pushed away from the mission ops console as the ship was rocked again.

"We can't stay in here much longer, Cap," shouted Casey. "We're getting pummeled harder than a journeyman boxer."

"Just hang on long enough for Blake to get a shot at those rocks," said Taylor, practically falling into the command chair, "get close and then give him manual control."

"Aye aye, Captain Taylor Ray," Casey replied, and then began to weave the ship through the increasingly savage hailstorm of rocks and asteroid fragments. "Blake, now's the time to make good on your bragging. You have control in three, two, one, go!"

Blake grabbed the manual firing column and was then tied into thruster control so that wherever he aimed, the ship pointed. Another deep thud resonated throughout the hull and alarms rang out.

"Hull breach!" shouted James over the din, "Cargo hold... it's contained..."

"Any time now, Blake!" cried Taylor, but Blake Meade was as still as a crouching tiger and just as ready to strike. He flicked the column in steady movements, lining up the nose of the ship with the target, and then fired.

The cannon shells sped out ahead and lit up the cluster of rocks that James had targeted, causing an explosion at least ten times more energetic than cannons alone could ever produce. The explosion encompassed adjacent asteroids and began a cascade that raced directly towards the Corvus cruiser.

"Did we get it?" shouted Taylor. The view port was saturated by a succession of vivid explosions, making it difficult to see whether the enemy ship had been consumed, along with the asteroids.

James peered down at his console, "Unclear, I'm still detecting a ship out there. It could be damaged."

Then the bright flashes died away and the dust began to clear, but through it Taylor could still see the tank-like outline of the Corvus-class cruiser. He checked the console in his chair and slammed his fist down, accidentally denting the arm due to his superhuman strength. "Damn it, it moved away, it must have seen what we were planning!"

"Smart li'l ship;" said Blake, also checking his screens, "it took some damage, but it's a tough nut to crack. It's not outta the fight yet."

"And we may have just given it an idea..." said James, ominously.

The rest of the crew all turned to face him in near perfect synchronization. "What do you mean?" said Taylor, knowing that whatever the answer was, it wasn't good.

"Some of the asteroids surrounding our current position have the same mineral composition."

Taylor looked to Casey, but she was already looking at him, wide eyed. She didn't need Taylor to give the order; she knew they had to get out of the asteroid field, smartly.

"Hang on to your hats!" Casey shouted, pulling the pilot's view port closer and grabbing the consoles, "This might get a bit turbulent."

"Enemy ship's firin', Cap!" Blake called out, as plasma shards flashed past, detonating the unstable asteroids that were now vanishing to their aft, thanks to Casey's quick reactions. The ship shuddered and conduits blew out around them, flooding the bridge with acrid smoke.

"Minor damage to secondary systems. Repair drones on site," coughed James. "Enabling bridge vents, now!"

Taylor's lack of lungs and simulant eyes meant the smoke had no effect on him, other than to obscure the viewport. He stood and ran up beside Blake, "I've had enough of this," he said, placing a hand on Blake's back, "Take it down; your discretion."

"You got it, Cap," Blake replied, then he transmitted an attack plan that he'd already been cooking up over to Casey's console, "Hey, Casey, can you pull that off?" He shouted over to her.

Casey didn't look away from her viewport, but gave a thumbs up and shouted back, "Ain't nothing to it, Blakey!"

Blake and Taylor glanced at each other, smiling, and then Taylor returned to the command chair. "You have control, Tactical Specialist Meade."

Smaller plasma shards from the cruiser's turrets raked across the hull, causing more conduits to overload, but Casey was now almost clear of the asteroid field and had placed one of the larger hulks of rock between them and the enemy cruiser. She brought their ship to a stop, only meters away from the asteroid's surface, noting that the enemy cruiser changed course and tracked to the side in an effort to bring them back into a weapons arc. But Casey had already begun to climb over the asteroid, skimming the surface and keeping the bulk of the asteroid between them and the enemy, which was now aiming its cannons in completely the wrong place. Casey drew her eyes out of the viewport and looked over at Blake.

"Ready?"

Blake nodded and took hold of the manual firing controls, with a deftness of touch that belied his inelegant mannerisms and stocky frame, which had not diminished even in simulant form.

Casey peered back into the viewport and then maneuvered the ship over the top of the asteroid, orbiting it at a velocity that shouldn't have been possible without crashing into one of its many jagged outcroppings, and brought them out above their enemy, like a bird of prey, ready to swoop on an unsuspecting vole.

Blake opened fire with the cannons, striking the enemy cruiser on its aft quarter, pulverizing its engines and tearing open the hull. Then as Casey soared above it, he raked the ventral section with turret fire, filling it with more holes than a colander. Micro detonations erupted all across the ship and then a powerful internal detonation ripped it in two.

James leapt from his seat and whooped, "Yeah, we got it! Woohoo!", but then looked deeply embarrassed, as the simulator lights blinked on, and the consoles all shut down, leaving only the echo of his exuberant yell lingering in the air.

Then from the back of the simulator, there came a steady clap, clap, clap.

"I must admit, that was a very impressive performance," said Commander Sonner, stepping out of the shadows. "One worthy of a whoop..." she added, winking at her brother, whose cheeks flushed red.

"How long have you been there?" asked Taylor turning to face her.

"Long enough to know that this is one hell of a combat crew," said Sonner. "I wish we had ninety-nine more of you."

"No way," said Blake, climbing out from his station, "one Captain Taylor Ray is enough, and I don't like the idea of other Blakes runnin' around the place, either.

"The human crews will do just fine," said Taylor, ignoring Blake. "This simulator is good. In fact, it's way tougher than I expected."

"That's because I ramped the difficulty level up to maximum," said Sonner, not even attempting to hide her amusement.

"Well, I hope the Hedalt crews aren't all as good as these simulated ones," Taylor replied, failing to see the funny side, "because they won't all be flying those older Corvus cruisers. And our rust-bucket of a Corvette won't be much use against the bigger frigates."

"Hey, Cap, don't talk about the Contingency One like that," said Casey, scowling at him. "I'd take our ship over a War Frigate any day of the week. We've gotten the best of those brutes before."

"And you will have to again, and maybe even worse," Sonner cut back in. "Sooner than you think."

Taylor's brow furrowed, "What do you mean? We're still running the various crews though the simulators, and we've yet to start the field trials."

Sonner stepped further onto the bridge and folded her arms, "I'm afraid our new commander in chief has others ideas," she said, now with a cold soberness. "He wants to move on Earth as soon as possible, and using the original battle plans."

"He's gotta be outta his damn mind!" exclaimed Blake. "Those plans're staler than the Cap's underpants."

Casey let out a bellicose laugh, but Taylor was not amused.

"That's one way of putting it," said Sonner, more than a little disturbed by Blake's vivid analogy, "but, thankfully, the five of us are quite sane."

"What do you have in mind?" asked Taylor, now understanding the reason why she had been lurking this whole time.

"Collins may be an idiot, but he is the senior officer," Sonner began, "and he'll relieve me from duty if I bust his balls any more than I already have been. So we have to follow his dumbass orders, even if they're the wrong ones."

"But..." said Taylor, expectantly.

"But that doesn't mean we have to sit on our hands," said Sonner, "we can still improvise."

Taylor's simulant eyes raised up, "What exactly do you mean by 'improvise'?"

A loud laugh from Blake took the place of Sonner's reply, as he casually strolled up beside Taylor. "She means we're gonna have to break the rules an' go rogue," he said, smiling broadly. Then he sauntered towards the exit, slapping Sonner on the shoulder as he passed. "Maybe I like her after all..."

TWENTY-NINE

A strong aroma of coffee wafted down the central corridor of the Contingency One and distracted Taylor from his intended plan of returning to his quarters to regenerate. He doubled back to the mess hall and poked his head around the corner to see Sonner busy at the counter, though he couldn't quite see what she was doing, as her back was shielding his view. It had piqued his interest enough to want to nose around some more.

"If didn't know better, I'd say you were up to no good," he said, leaning against the frame of the archway.

Taylor's sudden announcement caused Sonner to jump and then yelp in pain. She peered back at him, crossly, "Damn it, Taylor, you made me burn my damn wrist," she said, shaking her right hand vigorously. "Haven't you learned how to knock yet?"

Taylor shrugged and then looked at the open archway. "There's no door." Sonner had instructed her drones to remove it when building the mess hall in order to give the space a more 'communal vibe', as she had put it.

"What are you doing here, anyway?" Sonner went on, obviously still cross with him. "You don't eat."

"And you're grumpy when you've not had enough coffee," Taylor hit back, moving further into the hall. "I assume that's what you're doing with that mad science kit you have there?" Taylor was looking at the strange contraption that Sonner had set up on the counter, which looked like a school chemistry set.

"It's a coffee siphon, actually," growled Sonner, "it's an ancient method of brewing coffee so that it actually tastes good, unlike the crap that comes out of that machine." She pointed with her scalded hand to the food processor perched on the far edge of the counter. "I brought one with me before I went into stasis."

"Glad to see you had your priorities straight…" said Taylor with a whiff of sarcasm, but Sonner had returned her attention to the device and ignored him. Taylor moved closer and studied the elaborate array of glass chambers and what looked like an actual naked flame to heat the water and then just looked at Sonner as if she was a genuine mad scientist. "Seems like a lot of effort just for a hot drink."

"Yeah, well, to your simulant taste buds, maybe," she snapped.

Clearly, questioning Sonner's coffee rituals was a subject to be avoided. She finally turned off the flame, waited for the dark brown liquid to filter through into the lower flask and then poured it into a bright red mug.

Taylor noticed that the mug had letters printed on the side and he shifted position so he could read them. "Keep Calm And Drink Coffee?" he said out loud, reading the words on the mug.

"That's what I'm trying to do..." said Sonner, blowing gently over the lip of the mug before taking a few sips, which seemed to have an instant soothing effect on her frayed nerves.

"So am I now talking to Dr Jekyll instead of Mr. Hyde?" Taylor asked, smirking.

"Very funny," said Sonner after another longer slurp, thought she was now notably more relaxed and significantly less snarky. "Your literary references never fail to amuse."

"Well, after what you told me earlier, if I didn't laugh I'd probably cry," said Taylor, pulling up a chair at a nearby table and sitting down. "Not that

I have any tear ducts."

Sonner drew up a chair and sat down next to him, stretching out her legs underneath the table and cradling the red mug in both hands, as if it was some kind of sacred artifact. There was silence for a few seconds and then Sonner said, "You were right about him. Collins, I mean."

"It was a lucky guess," replied Taylor. He wasn't surprised that Sonner had admitted this so freely; she may have been stubborn, but she wasn't prideful. "Or an unlucky guess, as it turns out."

"We need to know what we're dealing with," continued Sonner, "which means we need to know how well Earth is defended."

"Fortunately, I know someone who might be able to help..." said Taylor, knowing full well where Sonner was headed, though he'd come to the same conclusion himself. Despite the growing dangers of him entering the Fabric, both in terms of the personal risk, and the prospect that Provost Adra might track his location and discover their base, he knew he would need to head through the starlight door again. He would need to go to Earth.

Sonner took another sip of her coffee. "But with our new friend watching me like a foreman, and our old friend in black armor still out there looking for us, it's not going to be easy."

"If it *was* easy, it wouldn't be any fun," Taylor replied, with a rebelliousness that was worthy of

Casey Valera.

Sonner didn't respond, but Taylor could see in her eyes that she felt the same way. There was silence between them for a few moments, punctuated only by the sound of Sonner sipping her coffee.

"I meant what I said about your crew," said Sonner, with more than half the mug already drained. "It's a truly exceptional team. You should be proud."

Taylor sighed, "I don't think I can really take any credit," he said, and then he tapped his head, "It's all in the programming."

"It's more than that, and you know it," Sonner replied, "The connection you all have can't be engineered. It's something special. It's what makes you human." Then she smirked, "Well, part robot, part human, anyway."

"Thankfully, this robot's feelings can't be hurt," Taylor answered. "Sticks and stones, remember?"

"I hope you remember that the next time we meet our charming Provost friend again," Sonner replied, with a teacherly tone, and Taylor returned a conciliatory nod.

There was silence for a few more seconds, until Taylor spoke up. "You're a part of this crew too, you know. Me, Casey, Blake... we'd all still be having our strings pulled by those gray-skinned psychos if it wasn't for you."

Sonner smiled at him. "We haven't finished reassembling the crew, remember? There's still one more we have to find." Then she looked at him with a cold seriousness. "And we *will* find her, Taylor. I promise you, we will."

Satomi Rose... thought Taylor, though in truth thoughts of her were rarely far from his mind. He told himself that the Satomi he'd spoken to in the Fabric was still out there. But it was hard to shake the memory of Provost Adra literally tearing the head off the Satomi simulant from Blake's ship. He still held out hope, but he also had to consider the possibility that Provost Adra had destroyed the last Satomi Rose unit in the galaxy.

"You're right, I'm sure we'll find her," he said, half-smiling. *Glass half-full...* "She's the only real family I have, along with Casey and Blake." Then he returned Sonner's serious stare. "And you too, Sarah."

Sonner looked away, but not because she was embarrassed. She seemed suddenly sad.

"I'm sorry," said Taylor, worried that he'd offended her somehow, "I didn't mean to..."

"It's not that," Sonner interrupted. Then she swallowed hard and looked into his eyes again. "On the reserve base, when we were running through the names of those who had survived hibernation, and you pointed out Collins... well... I thought you were pointing out someone else."

"Who?" Taylor was mesmerized by Sonner's sudden confession.

"My ex-husband." Taylor recoiled so hard he almost fell of his chair. "He's one of the flight crew. A captain, actually."

Taylor grabbed the back of his neck, astonished by the news. "Well, have you spoken to him?"

"No."

"Why the hell not?" Taylor asked, almost too aggressively. He could see Sonner's eyes harden and her armor start to return, so he backed down. "I'm sorry, I know it's not my business, but hell, if there was ever a reason for forgiveness and second chances... Even if it's just a second chance at a friendship. There aren't many of us left, Sarah."

"It's complicated," replied Sonner, taking another sip of coffee.

"It always is."

"And we didn't part on the best of terms," Sonner added, half hiding behind her mug.

Taylor sighed and then smiled. "Well, they say time is a great healer, and you've both had more than three hundred years and I don't know how many thousands of light years apart. So who knows. Glass half-full, right?"

Sonner laughed and then raised her mug, "Well, I'll drink to your optimism, if nothing else," she said, before draining the last of the coffee. Then she got up and placed the mug delicately onto the counter, before stopping by Taylor's side and resting a hand gently on his shoulder. "We'll talk again soon, Captain. Rest well, you've earned it."

"Aye aye, Commander Sarah Sonner," Taylor replied, offering a casual salute.

Taylor remained at the table for a few minutes after Sonner had gone, thinking about everything that had happened since they had last set out from the Contingency base. From the rescue of the flight crews, to facing Provost Adra in the flesh, saving and waking up Blake, and the new problem of Colonel Collins, it had been one hell of a roller coaster. But he was also acutely aware of how close they'd come to falling off the rails. Provost Adra had them dead to rights and for whatever reason she had let them go. But if there was one thing he'd never been more sure of in his short, real life, it was that he'd meet Provost Adra again.

Suddenly, his head felt wooly and weary and he remembered why he had come back onto the Contingency One in the first place, which was to go to bed and regenerate. He got up, pushed the two chairs – his and Sonner's – neatly back under the table and turned to leave. He shot one last glance back at Sonner's array of drinks-making equipment on the counter and smiled. *Keep Calm And Drink Coffee...* he said, reminding himself of the motto on Sonner's mug. *If only it were that simple.*

THIRTY

Taylor sat on the edge of his bed and picked up the data pad from the table by its side. He flipped it over in his hands for a few seconds, trying to distill the millions of thoughts that were racing through his mind. The ship's logs and mission reports had already detailed the facts of the events, but it was all so sterile and anemic. Instead, he wanted to record his feelings, while they were still vivid in his mind, which was as prone to forgetting things as any human brain was. Then, maybe another three hundred years down the line, if anyone survived the war to come, his journal might help others to understand the extraordinary times he lived in. The fight for the survival of the human race, as told through the silver eyes of a simulant. He stopped flipping the pad over and then logged into the account, 'Taylor Ray - Awake'.

Personal Journal - Entry #3

It's terrifying to think that this journal entry was almost never written. This time we only scraped through by the skin of our teeth, and even then it was perhaps more through luck than judgement. But we made it back and I guess that's all that matters in the end. No, scratch that... We didn't just come back – we came back stronger. *That's* what matters.

We already had the warships, and thanks to Sonner's engineering geniuses, they're as good as new. The irony is they're also more than a little long in the tooth, compared to what's out there waiting for us. But this brand new, out-of-date fleet of ninety-nine Nimrods is all we have, and so it will have to be enough.

And now, thanks to another lucky roll of the dice, we have flight crews. Are we ready? Not even close. Many of them are as showroom-fresh as the Nimrods. But maybe that was the best we could ever hope for, and some hope is always better than none.

But while our fortunes have improved in some ways, in others our situation has become far more precarious. Our enemy knows we're out here and she'll be looking for us. She knows our faces and she knows our ship. Whether out here in the vast expanse or inside the sub-layer of space that is the Fabric, sooner or later she'll find us. Maybe it's a good thing. I know I'm tired of skulking around and hiding and running. It's time we took the fight to them.

Of course, it's not that easy, because it's not only the threat of the Hedalt we have to contend with. As our family has grown lager, so has it become more dysfunctional. There's a black sheep in every flock and ours is Colonel Chester Collins. I had a feeling he was bad news, and I've never been more sorry to be right. But we'll work it out. We'll have to, because the stakes are too high to allow one individual – no matter whether it's a man, woman or simulant – to threaten the success of the entire Contingency. Because if we lose, we die. And I don't want to die, because I'm just getting used to being alive.

It helps that I'm no longer alone. Casey and Blake are the same as me, and in a strange way that makes them family. Blake and I have always had a love/hate relationship – he loved to push my buttons and I hated it – but having him around again just feels right. It's like a part of me returned that I didn't even know was missing. I'm also a little jealous of how easily he adjusted to his new simulant reality, but I guess I should have expected nothing less from Blake. He always saw the universe through a heavily polarized lens. And he's lucky too, because he still has the one person in the universe he cares about the most. Was his love for Casey a part of the original Blake Meade's past or invented by the Hedalt? Who knows, but if I had to choose, I'd choose to believe it was real. Something so true and so honest couldn't be faked. But I guess it doesn't matter either way. This Casey and Blake are alive and their feelings are as real and as unshakable as the rock surrounding this base.

Thinking about family always brings me back to Satomi Rosc. I worry that when I close my eyes, all I'll see is Adra tearing her apart and tossing her aside like a worthless piece of trash. In my simulant body, my emotions are contained and constrained, but in my dreams, the pain is real and agonizing. I try to be optimistic, but I've never been one to live on false hopes. I know I may never see her again, and I know I'll never truly be complete if I don't.

None of it matters if we don't win this war; not Satomi or Blake or Casey or Sonner, or the hundreds of people on this base – all that remains of humanity in the universe. But I know we can win. I know, because I saw my enemy bleed. I saw her on her knees. So what if they have superior numbers? So what if they have superior ships? That's just math, and it takes more than that to win a war. When it comes down to it, I know they can be beaten. We may not be as formidable a fighting force as King Leonidas and his three hundred Spartans, but our will to win is just as strong. Hopefully, history will show that we had a better outcome.

One hundred ships against an Empire. It sounds crazy, but it might just work. One way or another, this will be Earth's last war.

The end.

TO BE CONTINUED...

The Contingency War Series will conclude in the final book, Earth's Last War.

Earth's Last War:

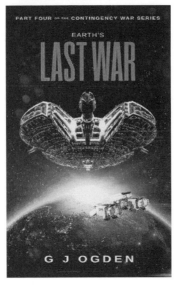

All the books in the series:

- The Contingency
- The Waystation Gambit
- Rise of Nimrod Fleet
- Earth's Last War

ALSO BY THIS AUTHOR

If you enjoyed this book, please consider reading The Planetsider Trilogy, also by G J Ogden. Available from Amazon and free to read for Kindle Unlimited subscribers.

The Planetsider Trilogy:
A post-apocalyptic thriller with a military Sci-Fi twist

- **The Planetsider**

- **The Second Fall**

- **The Last of the Firsts**

*"The strong action sequences and thoughtful worldbuilding make this one worth picking up for fans of plot-driven SF." - **Publishers Weekly***

ABOUT THE AUTHOR

At school I was asked to write down the jobs I wanted to do as a 'grown up'. Number one was astronaut and number two was a PC games journalist. I only managed to achieve one of those goals (I'll let you guess which), but these two very different career options still neatly sum up my lifelong interests in science, space and the unknown.

School also steered me in the direction of a science-focused education over literature and writing, which influenced my decision to study physics at Manchester University. What this degree taught me is that I didn't like studying physics and instead enjoyed writing, which is why you're reading this book! The lesson? School can't tell you who you are.

When not writing, I enjoy spending time with my family, walking in the British countryside, and indulging in as much Sci-Fi as possible.

You can connect with me here:
https://twitter.com/GJ_Ogden
https://www.facebook.com/PlanetsiderNovel

Subscribe to my newsletter:
http://subscribe.ogdenmedia.net